"DID YOU KNOW YOU LOOK LIKE A PRINCESS?"

Lucy blushed. This wasn't the first time someone had called her a princess, but she'd never felt like one until this moment. There was a fullness of affection in the way the name rolled off the earl's lips, causing her heart to melt and her pulse to quicken.

He reached out and touched her cheek, his fingertips brushing her lips. He whispered, "I should like to kiss you. You know that, don't you?"

Lucy could scarcely breathe, no less utter a reply.

"And would you like that?" was his enticing query.

She had to swallow before she could speak. "Yes," she said.

"You must come closer," he murmured.

Other Regency Romances from Avon Books

MISS WICKHAM'S BETROTHAL

NANCY RICHARDS-AKERS

AVON BOOKS ◆ NEW YORK

MISS WICKHAM'S BETROTHAL is an original publication of Avon Books. This work has never before appeared in book form. This work is a novel. Any similarity to actual persons or events is purely coincidental.

AVON BOOKS
A division of
The Hearst Corporation
1350 Avenue of the Americas
New York, New York 10019

Copyright © 1992 by Nancy Richards-Akers
Published by arrangement with the author
Library of Congress Catalog Card Number: 92-90137
ISBN: 0-380-76532-2

First Avon Books Printing: September 1992

AVON TRADEMARK REG. U.S. PAT. OFF. AND IN OTHER COUNTRIES, MARCA REGISTRADA, HECHO EN U.S.A.

Printed in the U.S.A.

RA 10 9 8 7 6 5 4 3 2 1

To my parents with my love and best wishes
for many years of happiness in your new life
on your lovely island

With thanks to Amanda Potts, Molly Manning,
Maria Del Castillo, and Karen McCray

So he swam to the buoy and the little waves danced,
And the sea breeze freshly blew;
And the old buoy danced and the shadows of the clouds
Raced over the bay and flew.

But he found no playmates on the buoy,
And he thought of those girls so sweet.
Then he longed and he longed in his loneliness now
Some other water babies for to meet.

CHARLES KINGSLEY, *Water Babies*

Prologue

❀ ❀ ❀ ❀

1807

"**I** BELIEVE I'D LIKE TO MARRY YOU, sir, if you please," the child declared. She stood in a shallow tidal pool, her jonquil-yellow frock tucked into damp pantaloons, seawater lapping at her bare ankles. The expression upon her upturned countenance was entirely serious as she awaited the gentleman's reply.

"Was that a proposal?"

"Indeed, sir." She raised a hand to shade her eyes from the August sun and better view the gentleman. He was tall. Indeed, he was the tallest man she'd ever known and certainly the most handsome, with hair as black as midnight, eyes as blue as the summer sea, and strong masculine features that reminded her of the pirate king she'd seen in a picture book in Reverend Addison's library. The girl smiled and her eyes twinkled with delight, for the notion of being a pirate's wife was vastly appealing to her. "Will you marry me?"

The object of this heartfelt proposal tossed back his head and surrendered to deep resounding laughter that rose above the crash of incoming waves. "And your father, my dear minx, would have me drawn and quartered for allowing you to entertain such a flight of fancy. If you were to ask anyone, they'd tell you my reputation is tarnished quite beyond redemption. Not a favorable match, I assure you."

The girl's lips pursed into a perfect bow as she contemplated his response. She hadn't anticipated a rejection. After all, he was her best friend, and it had never occurred to her that he might consider himself unworthy.

"My father's dead, y'know, and there's no one else to disapprove what I do." Placing her hands on her hips, she gave a definitive nod as if to agree with herself. This sharp movement caused her straw bonnet to tumble off her head and dangle down her back by its ribbons, but she didn't bother to put it back on. This speech was much more important. "There's only Headmistress and Mr. Bradshaw, Papa's solicitor, but he's in London, and all either of them really care is whether I spend more than my monthly stipend allows. I don't believe they'd mind one jot whom I married. Not one jot. Besides which, I don't care for other people's opinions anyway."

He frowned at the defiant tilt of her chin. Until that moment he hadn't known the full extent of her situation. Although he'd realized she didn't spend holidays with family, he'd assumed it was because her parents were posted in Bermuda or Kuala Lumpur or some such distant place. To know beyond a doubt that this delightful girl was alone in the world was sobering, and of a sudden, he sensed that she was much more vulnerable than she allowed herself to appear. In his kindest manner, he said, "Be that as it may, dear minx, you're still far too young for me."

"But you must admit I've grown up since last

summer.'' She made a full turn in the tidal pool. ''Like Jack's bean pole, says Headmistress. Why, I've already had two new wardrobes this year. It's my arms and legs, y'see, growing far too fast. You don't think I shall be a giant, do you? I wouldn't like that. To be a giant. It's not in the least bit ladylike, and I do think it must be grand to be a lady.''

This brought a fond glimmer to the gentleman's blue eyes. The first time he'd encountered the girl had been three years before. It had been his initial visit to Battersea Hall, and he was walking along the beach when he'd noticed a sodden mass being spat upon the shore by a wave. Clearly, it was a child, sputtering and in distress, and he'd rushed to the rescue, hardly realizing that the tiny figure he scooped up was female, a young boarding student from the nearby school. His hostess, Lady Anne, had insisted that the girl be dispatched to the headmistress, who had delivered the chit a most tremendous scold in their presence. Apparently, however, the dressing-down produced no lasting effect, for the next day there she was again, scampering down the beach, barefoot, dodging in and out of the waves and trying her hardest to swim.

That first summer, he'd taught the girl to swim. The second summer, he'd included her on several sailing expeditions, and this summer, they'd added fishing to their list of pastimes. From her, he'd learned about trust and how to laugh without pretense, and she'd imparted a priceless eagerness to enjoy life to its fullest.

She'd grown since that first August, from a stubborn child to a delightful companion, and of late, he'd even noticed signs of budding womanhood. Indeed, he often found himself imagining what an intriguing woman she would surely become. Yet when that might be was a mystery, for he hadn't the vaguest notion how old she was. He didn't even know her name. He'd called her Minx from the first moment he'd fished her from the surf; she called him Pip, his childhood nickname; and they called this sandy stretch of coastline their special meeting place.

"Are you going to marry *her?*" The minx glanced up the cliff to where Lady Anne was sitting beneath a makeshift shelter of blue-and-white-striped canvas.

Lady Anne loathed the sun, loathed the wind, and loathed anything that didn't take place beneath a satin counterpane. Thank God he'd met the girl and had had such a pleasurable distraction from Lady Anne during these visits to Battersea Hall. As satisfying as his amorous hostess might be, even the most lustful gentleman couldn't devote all his energies to servicing her carnal appetites.

"No, I'm not going to marry Lady Anne," he said, thinking that while she was a delicious mistress, she'd make a hideously unfaithful wife.

"That's good." The girl was smiling again, an adorable impish grin that made her green eyes sparkle and her petal-pink cheeks dimple. "I don't like her one iota. She's prodigiously spoilt, and, y'know, Pip, I think she likes to gamble," she added in a theatrical whisper.

Again, he laughed. "And how, dear minx, would you come to know something like that?"

"I overheard her talking with Lord Grayson. She owes him eighteen pounds for losses at whist, and five more because she said someone named Clarissa Rushton's hair was dyed a dreadful shade of red, but he brought her proof it's not."

"Ah." He grinned.

Several moments passed. The girl stood on one foot while she swished the water about with her other. "If not me, then who shall you marry?"

"I hadn't planned on marrying anyone. At least not for a while."

This time, she beamed with happiness. "Oh, I'm so very glad to hear that, sir, for when I'm all grown up, I plan to make you change your mind about me."

"Ah, then, as a gentleman I could do no less than to wait for you to grow up." With much flourish he performed a courtly bow and offered a roguish grin as he entertained the wholly improper notion that once grown this enchanting green-eyed minx would have a host of gentlemen considering matrimony—and, in particular, the intimate prerogatives it entailed.

His answer thrilled her, and next August, when Battersea Hall was opened and the entourage of carriages from London wheeled down the lane, a slender girl slipped over the orchard wall at the Royal Brighton Academy for Young Ladies and rushed down to the beach to wait for Pip. She was three inches taller, her hair, once rather thin and ratty in appearance, had thickened and turned a glorious shade of gold, and she had a figure, a development which was certain to convince him she was finally old enough to be taken seriously.

But he hadn't accompanied Lady Anne to Battersea Hall. This time, she was escorted by a rather stout gentleman who carried a quizzing glass, and the following summer there was an attentive Irish earl by her side. After that, the girl never returned to the special meeting place again.

One

1813

PRINCESS WAS THE AFFECTIONATE NICKNAME given Miss Lucy Wickham by her classmates at the Royal Brighton Academy for Young Ladies. In point of fact, Rascal might have suited better, for the willowy golden-haired girl with great green eyes owned a deplorable penchant for the most hoydenish behavior. The Princess preferred fishing to practicing her scales on the pianoforte and climbing trees to Tuesday lessons with the dancing master, and on more than one occasion, she had been the ringleader when salt was substituted for sugar in the refectory kitchen or when a family of hedgehogs was smuggled into the Reverend Addison's sitting room. Furthermore, there wasn't an ounce of royal blood in Miss Lucy Wickham's veins but her manner of arrival at the academy had been most regal, and that sufficed as adequate justification.

Unlike most girls, who were escorted to school by their mothers or some other respectable female relative, Miss Lucy had arrived in the company of a Scots governess, a French maid, two Connemara ponies, and a groom; unlike the other boarding students, who shared rooms in the dormitory, Miss Lucy and her entourage were housed in a private cottage at the end of the cherry orchard; unlike the other girls, whose school wardrobes were limited to sensible dresses in shades of gray and brown, Miss Lucy's allowance provided for a stylish new wardrobe with each season.

Now it appeared her departure from the academy was to be equally as noteworthy as her arrival.

"You wished to see me, Headmistress?" Lucy inquired after a polite good-morning and quick curtsy.

"Please, be seated." The plump woman who was seated behind a kneehole dressing table that served as a desk smiled with genuine affection as she indicated a chair situated in a sunny spot by the window. It had been eleven years since the Princess had come to the academy, and Mrs. Baldwin rather thought of her as a daughter, a very special daughter who had blossomed from an unremarkable child into a beautiful young lady whose unfailing generosity and kindness of heart had provided a celebratory party complete with fancy cake and gifts ordered from the Burlington Arcade for every soul upon their birthday while residing within the six-acre compound known as the Royal Brighton Academy for Young Ladies. No one from the eldest teacher to the lowliest scullery maid had ever been forgotten by the Princess, and everyone had been more than willing to resort to one or another tiny white lie when the Princess was about one of her escapades.

"Y'know, my dear child, in previous years, a summons to my quarters was more than likely prelude to a reprimand for some prank or indiscretion of yours.''

Lucy blushed demurely, sat a bit straighter, and smoothed out the skirt of her muslin gown. The dress was one of her more sedate ones, in a shade of dove gray with a wide lace ruffle about the high collar and cuffs. When she'd been informed that Headmistress wished to see her, Lucy had chosen this particular dress with great care. Of late, she'd been trying exceedingly hard to be more ladylike. Although her classmates had graduated last spring, Lucy had remained at the academy in a peculiar status that was neither student nor teacher. Verily, the afternoon the other girls departed had been the saddest of her life, sadder even than when Papa had died, for she had been very young then and the prospect of being shipped off to boarding school had seemed a marvelous adventure. At the age of seventeen, however, the prospect of remaining at the Royal Brighton Academy in perpetuity was sobering in the extreme, for it offered no future, no adventures, and most important of all, there was no chance of realizing her fondest dream within the confines of its five-foot-high stucco walls.

Unlike the other girls, Lucy did not wish to attain celebrity as one of London's Incomparables and ensnare the realm's most eligible duke, nor did she wish to travel to the exotic reaches of the world or become a bluestocking and devote her days to literature and natural history. Lucy's fondest wish was to become a mother and be surrounded by the love and sharing and companionship which she imagined was part and parcel of parenthood. Sometimes late at night when she pondered her situation she could not help wondering if she were to blame. No one liked a hoyden, and if she ever hoped to go out into the world and have a family of her own, she must turn over a new leaf and behave like a well-bred young lady. For the umpteenth time, she apologized to Headmistress. "I did not mean to trouble you, ma'am."

Mrs. Baldwin waved a hand to prevent Lucy saying another word. "Now, my dear child, there shall be none of that. You are much grown up this past year, and when all is said and done we shall always remember you with nothing but the fondest of memories."

"Remember me?" Lucy's heart leapt in hopeful anticipation.

"Indeed. Mr. Bradshaw has written his customary letter, and this time he conveys the most splendid news. Arrangements have been made for your come-out this Season in London." From the desk she picked up a sheet of vellum stationery and perused it as if to confirm the contents. "It appears your father's will stipulated that upon your eighteenth birthday a sponsor would be found to insure a suitable match. Do you remember Lady Margaret Mersham?"

Of course, she did. Lady Margaret had been one of Lucy's classmates, both of the girls having begun their school careers at the age of seven, and Lucy replied with an affirmative nod, hardly daring to utter a single syllable, for fear this moment and this wonderful news would evaporate as did a pleasant afternoon dream upon waking.

"Knowing you had spent one Christmas with her family, Mr. Bradshaw deemed it logical to discuss the terms of your father's will with Lady Margaret's parents, and having done so, her mother, the Countess of Mersham, has agreed to take you under her wing for a Season. As you may know, Lady Margaret was wed last September, and the countess's other daughters are still in the nursery."

Lucy gave another silent nod as she thought of Margaret and her army of siblings—four brothers and three sisters, to be exact—and her soft-spoken mother. It was that Christmas with Lady Margaret's family that had filled the lonely little girl's heart with dreams, and the prospect of once more visiting that merry family, not to mention having a London Season, was more than Lucy ever thought to imagine.

"Great goose grease!" she exclaimed in a rather loud tenor, sounding like the village girl who came on Saturdays to wash the bed linens, and then remembering her pledge to behave like a lady, she lowered her voice. "I mean, I can hardly believe a word of this. Tell me, is it really true, ma'am? Oh, how truly lucky I am."

A momentary shadow crossed Mrs. Baldwin's face. Luck had nothing to do with it. Mr. Bradshaw had written that he had been forced to compensate the countess quite handsomely in exchange for her hospitality. Truth to tell, no one wished to sponsor a chit of unknown parentage, particularly a young lady who had inspired the tasteless appellation Princess. It was sinful how snobbish people could be, and it pained the headmistress deeply that Miss Lucy, their dear selfless Princess, had experienced more than her share of arrogance. The parents of the other students, with no consideration for the sensibilities of a lonely child, had not issued holiday invitations, nor had they included her in outings when they came to visit their daughters. With the single exception of that one December when she had traveled north to Castle Mersham with Lady Margaret, Lucy had passed every Christmas, every Easter, and every summer holiday with her governess and maid in the cottage at the edge of the cherry orchard without complaint. Headmistress had always stressed the virtue of spiritual fortitude to her girls, and Lucy had proven herself the strongest of them all.

"Oh, I just knew it," Lucy declared, happiness lighting her wide green eyes and bringing a delightful shade of high pink to her cheeks.

"Knew what, my dear child?"

"That I wouldn't be left here forever. That I hadn't been forgotten. Oh, please don't think me ungrateful, ma'am, for all that you've done for me, but I had begun to feel a bit awkward. So much older than the other girls and rather in your way after all these years."

Mrs. Baldwin waved a dismissive hand. "I quite understand, my dear child, and there's no need to explain. May I share a secret with you?" That affectionate smile prevailed. "I do believe I'm as thrilled as you are at this splendid opportunity. Verily, before the summer is concluded I expect to read an announcement in the *Times* that you've been betrothed to no less than a marquis."

"Oh, no, ma'am!"

"Why ever not?" Headmistress was perplexed. She'd never encountered a young lady who didn't yearn to acquire even the most modest title, but then dear Lucy wasn't like most young ladies.

"What I mean to say is that sort of thing—titles and such—they aren't important to me. I would be happy with anyone who would love me and wish to make me his wife."

"Well, I must say it's a relief to hear you shan't be picky. Many a young lady remains on the shelf not for want of offers but because of some misbegotten notion of matrimony and whom it is she wishes to wed.''

For the briefest instant, a distant memory flashed across Lucy's mind's eye. A pirate king with midnight-black hair and a laugh as full as the ocean on a stormy night. In the next instant, it was gone, replaced by the sights and sounds of Christmas dinner at Castle Mersham: a mother with tender words for all, a father watching his brood with a smile, teasing and laughing brothers and sisters, singing and chattering, and more love than Lucy had imagined there could be in any single place. She recalled the way the countess had dismissed her servants and had herself checked upon each child at bedtime, joining in as she and Lady Margaret said their evening prayers and then tucking the counterpane about them. How vivid was Lucy's recollection of the countess's lips quickly touching her forehead in a good-night kiss. And to think that sort of life was soon to be hers.

''Your father was a devoted parent, my dear child,'' Mrs. Baldwin impressed upon Lucy. ''Of course, I need not tell you that. His thoughtful will and your inheritance have enabled you to be with us these past years, but I feel duty bound to tell you that the management of your inheritance was intended to see you in good stead through school, a single Season, and to the altar. Mr. Bradshaw has asked me to explain that while a temporary account has been opened for you at a modiste in Mayfair and a small sum set aside for a dowry, should you not marry, the remaining funds would be insufficient to set up anything more than the most modest household.''

This intelligence did not dampen Lucy's exu-

berance, but mention of her father, as it always
did, caused small worry lines to appear upon her
brow. The extent of her knowledge of her father
was his name, Charles Drinker Wickham, and
that he'd perished on one of his frequent sea
voyages to the Far East. About her mother she
knew nothing. "Please, ma'am, might you be
able to tell me anything more about my father.
Or my mother? Perhaps he left a missive or
something to be opened upon my departure from
the academy."

"A missive, no. Something, yes." She pulled
open a drawer, withdrew a small leather box, and
standing, she walked around the desk to hand it
to Lucy. "Mr. Bradshaw included this with his
latest correspondence."

Tears filled Lucy's eyes as she accepted the box.
Her hands trembled. She knew it was silly of her
to react like this, but she couldn't help herself. So
much was happening at once, she could hardly
take it all in, and without wasting another moment she lifted the hinged lid to reveal a gold
locket resting upon black velvet. First, she
touched the locket, tentatively, merely allowing
her fingers to trace the delicate pattern of rose-
buds entwined with ivy, and after several moments, she turned it over and saw the inscription:
"C.E.A., 1796." Then she noticed a yellowed
piece of paper that had been folded into a small
square and stuffed into the top of the lid. Hoping
that whatever was written upon it might explain
the initials and date on the locket, she unfolded
the piece of paper.

It was a letter written to herself, and through a
veil of tears Lucy read the delicate curlicued
handwriting:

For my darling baby daughter, I have known you for but a fortnight, and every second of that brief time has been a mother's bliss. Each time you wrap your tiny hand about my finger my heart sings, and I do believe that was a smile upon your sweet face when Nurse brought you to me this morning. Sadly, if I am to believe the doctors, I fear we shall never know one another as I would wish, but I do own one small consolation in these final hours. Your father is firm in his belief that you look like me, and that notion gives me much comfort, for as I lie abed I can imagine your growing up by reliving memories of my own childhood.

My mother gave me this locket on the occasion of my comeout, and now I entrust it to your father. He has promised to give it to you when he takes you to London for your Season, and although I'm sure the dear man shall spoil you as dreadfully as he has me and shower you with all manner of frightfully costly jewels, I hope you shall choose to wear this locket next to your heart. My mother told me to fill it with pictures of my children, but that shall not be possible, so I fill it with my love and urge you to fill it with portraits of your babies. Eternally, Your loving mother.

A lump in her throat prevented Lucy from saying anything, and Mrs. Baldwin intervened. "Would you like me to help you put it on, my dear?"

"Yes, if you please, ma'am," she managed to reply, while one thought raced through her mind. *I look like her. I look like her. I look like her.* As soon as the locket lay against her chest she stood and crossed the room to stand before a mirror, pretending as she did that the tall young lady with wide green eyes and thick golden curls was her mother.

"Yes, Mother, I promise," Lucy whispered, her voice laced with determination and love. "I shall always wear your locket next to my heart, and soon I shall fill it with portraits of your grandchildren. I promise that both of our fondest wishes shall come true."

Two

ANTHONY PAGET, VISCOUNT DALSANY, had never experienced a more dismal start to a morning. That his head was splitting from the ill effects of too much brandy, that his mistress had left him for a gentleman plumper in the pockets, or that last evening he'd lost another hundred pounds to the hazard table at No. 77 Jermyn Street were the least of his worries.

He'd been aroused at the ungodly hour of ten by his valet to be informed that a gentleman by the name of Stern was calling about an outstanding loan. For the past several months, he'd managed to hold the duns at bay by referring them to his uncle, the Earl of Harrow. He was his uncle's sole heir, a prospect which generally placated the gullgropers and merchants seeking satisfaction for a mounting pile of unpaid bills. This morning, said explanation had succeeded with Mr. Stern, whereupon the viscount returned to the comfort of his bed only to be roused once again before another hour had elapsed.

This time, it was Mr. Samuel Frith, his uncle's solicitor, bringing, it would develop, the worst news the viscount had received in the whole of his twenty-two years.

"He's written another codicil to his will, you say," Dalsany drawled, but the waxen hue of his complexion belied this sanguine tone. Last year, his uncle had required that he attend some frightful series of lectures at the Royal Academy on agriculture and irrigation, after which he'd threatened to ship him off to the Caribbean to acquire firsthand experience at the family estate in Jamaica. "Damn the man, what the hell does he want from me now?"

The solicitor, who himself was looking rather pale, gave an awkward cough. "Well, sir, it appears your uncle has recently received several tradespersons who traveled to Clovelly Priory under the mistaken assumption that his lordship was responsible for your debts."

Apprehension settled upon the viscount's masculine features. Although less than ten years separated them in age, since being named his uncle's heir at the age of twenty, the viscount and the earl had been engaged in an ongoing disagreement about the younger gentleman's financial habits. Although profligate and addicted to the green baize, Dalsany was no fool, and he'd known that sooner or later the earl would cease to pay his vouchers. Fearing that regrettable hour had arrived, he hardly dared to ask:

"And what did my uncle do?"

"Well, sir, he sent for me to discuss how to best handle the situation."

The viscount frowned, jet-black brows arching in menacing fashion. "You're being rather circuitous, Frith. Ain't like you one jot. Whatever he's decided it can't be any worse than what's gone before." Loathing the notion of being vulnerable to another's whims, Dalsany forced a nonchalant shrug, then reached for the tapestry bell pull to summon his valet. "So there's another codicil. Well, out with it, man. What does he want from me now?"

"Would you like me to read it to you, sir?"

He gave an impatient wave. "No, don't bother to read all that legal mumbo jumbo. Just tell me the gist of it."

"It's very straightforward, sir. It's—Well, you see, sir—" The solicitor hesitated and emitted a second and no less awkward cough. Dalsany's unpredictable temperament was well known, and given the rather diabolical expression upon his darkening countenance, Mr. Frith took two steps backward before rushing on in revelation:

"Your uncle wishes that you marry, sir, and produce an offspring within the next eighteen months."

It was a good thing the viscount was already sitting, for Mr. Frith's statement had the momentary effect of robbing him of the ability to breathe. Whatever it was he had expected to hear this was hardly it. A sea voyage to some godforsaken colony, banishment to the countryside, a cut in his allowance, perhaps. But a wife and a child? The notion was unthinkable. What in heaven's name would he do with a wife and child?

"I say, Frith, can he do such a thing?" he demanded as his valet entered carrying a silver tray with a glass, two eggs each perched atop a Wedgwood eggcup, and a small carafe of dark liquid.

"Of course, anything he wishes, sir."

"Well, it ain't hardly fair," he remarked as he cracked the eggs into the glass and stirred in a few spoonfuls of the dark liquid. Done, he held the glass toward the window as if to inspect the quality of the mixture. Apparently, it wasn't quite right, and he stirred some more. "I mean the rea-

son he made me his heir in the first place was
because he's never married himself, and I don't
think it's in the least bit sporting of him to demand it of me."

"In anticipation of such a remark, his lordship
asked that I remind you that regardless of his
marital status, his conduct has, at no time, been
unbefitting to the title Earl of Harrow, nor a dis-
credit to the Paget name."

Dalsany gave a sober nod. That much was true.
His uncle was considered something of a saint,
and if he'd sown any wild oats, no one remembered those transgressions. All anyone knew was
that Alexander Paget, Earl of Harrow, former
ranking officer in the Royal Fusilier Brigade, was
a national hero, awarded numerous medals for
valor, and so gravely wounded in the Peninsular
War at Albuera that he'd been forced to quit his
command and retire to the family seat positioned
high above Lyme Bay near Weymouth on the
Dorset coast.

"Perhaps you'd like to read the precise lan-
guage, sir?"

"There's more bad news?" the viscount inquired before downing the contents of the glass
in a single swallow. "Raw egg and bitters, Frith,"
he remarked in an aside. "Works wonders. You
ought to try it sometime."

Frith grimaced, then addressed the viscount's
question. "Not bad news precisely, sir, but there
is the time limit to consider."

"Ah, yes, eighteen months, and I suppose if I
fail to do as the codicil dictates I shall be cut out
entirely."

"I'm afraid so, sir."

Having cogitated these facts for several moments, Dalsany arrived at the conclusion that

matters could have been far worse. The earl could have required that he enlist with the allied army on the Continent. If he was poor husband material, he was even less suited to a military career and would surely never have returned home to enjoy any inheritance. The viscount had been offered a chance to redeem himself, and he'd be a fool not to agree to the terms; the earl could very well have cut him out altogether without any second chance. Thus resigned to his fate, Dalsany asked, "Is there anything else I should know?"

"Just one detail. You must go to Clovelly for the wedding."

"Are you implying my uncle must approve my choice of bride?"

"No, sir, he merely wishes to be present at the ceremony and isn't sure he could make a trip."

The viscount's blue eyes flashed with cynical amusement. "Which is a polite way of saying he doesn't trust me and wishes to witness it for himself."

"I'm sure I couldn't say, sir."

Dalsany shrugged, stretched his long legs, and proceeded to inquire in an oddly matter-of-fact tone, "Tell me, Frith, how does one of Society's *mauvais sujets* go about finding a wife? I haven't had much contact with the polite world in recent years." Upon graduation from Cambridge, the viscount had briefly mingled with the ingenues and their mamas at Almack's, but since becoming the Paget heir his social life had centered around females of the demimonde and London's gambling halls. Once too often his name had been linked to one or another scandal. His reputation was notorious, his name synonymous with bad luck, and last autumn, the expression *Dalsanied* had been coined to refer to the dubious achieve-

ment of being evicted from one's lodgings owing
to bad debt. He couldn't remember the last time
he'd received an invitation from one of Mayfair's
more proper matrons.

"I suggest, sir, that you begin with the Dowager Duchess of Exeter."

"Excellent advice. I shall do that, Frith. Visit
the old gel at Berkeley Square, come clean, tell
her of my predicament, and pray for her good
graces."

The dowager duchess was Dalsany's great-aunt
on the distaff side, and a veritable social dragon
who might be persuaded to smooth over his in-
discretions and obtain a few invitations to the upcoming Season's festivities. If he was lucky, he
might even gain entree to Almack's, a ritual which
he found as distasteful as a visitation from a leech,
but which was probably unavoidable if he intended to secure a wife.

"I must say you're taking this quite well, sir."

"There's too much at stake here, and I'd be a
fool not to accept my uncle's terms." He grinned,
looking for all the world like the devil about to
embark on a mad scheme. "Anyway, Frith, who's
to say I won't fall madly in love? If I'm not mistaken, far stranger things have been known to
happen."

The Earl of Harrow stood on the cliff above
Lyme Bay, one hand raised to deflect the blaze of
the midday sun shining off the Channel waters.
As was his habit, he wore no hat, preferring instead to experience the sensation of the wind as
it tousled his hair. It reminded him of the times
when he'd been able to ride hell for leather across
the flats of the Dorset chalk, and it allowed him
for a brief space of time to feel again as if nothing

had changed, as if he were still whole and vigorous and future's every possibility was waiting to be his.

Only at times such as this did he regret his decision to name Dalsany his heir. It had seemed such an easy choice, not even his mother had been able to deter him, but now as he gazed from the headland to the down, all Paget lands as far as the eye could see, he wondered if he'd lost his mind. It was so achingly beautiful and for now it was his, and although naming Dalsany heir didn't alter that possession, it distanced the earl just that much further from the wellspring of life. And that, in point of fact, was what his decision had been all about.

Maimed by battle and disillusioned by a world turned upside down by greed and bloodshed, the Earl of Harrow had made the conscious decision not to marry to sire an heir. If there was one thing war had taught him it was that peace and happiness were by no means guaranteed, and so the Earl of Harrow had written his will and retired to Clovelly Priory on the wild Dorset coast. Of course, it made sense. It was what everyone expected a wounded soldier to do.

Three
❦ ❦ ❦ ❦

"**N**EVER THOUGHT YOU WERE SUCH A dreadful boy, Dalsany. Just a bit more impetuous than those Paget relatives would have it," the thin gray-haired lady pronounced upon being informed of the viscount's plight. They were seated in the dining room at one end of an immense mahogany table. Dalsany had arrived while the dowager duchess was at breakfast, and she had insisted that he join her. Although her grace never rose before eleven, she always had a hearty breakfast, and the table was a clutter of presentations from shirred eggs and porridge to kippers and sausage. "You always did remind me more of *our* side of the family. In fact, your behavior puts me in mind of your grandfather, my dear brother, Edgar."

"Thank you, your grace," replied the viscount, suspecting such a comparison—no matter how affectionate the phrasing—wasn't really much in the way of a compliment. The elderly lady's next statement confirmed that suspicion.

"Poor Edgar never was able to hold on to his funds. Bless him. Terrible weakness for hazard, y'know." She gave a sad nod toward a life-sized portrait hanging in an alcove at the far end of the dining room.

Dalsany popped another forkful of kippers into his mouth and peered at the oil painting of his mother's father. The fair-haired, fine-featured gentleman appeared to have been about Dalsany's age when the likeness was commissioned. He'd never known the gentleman, who broke his neck while in pursuit of a fox long before Dalsany was born, and having been raised by his father's family, the viscount had heard little of the gentleman's character. The mention of E.O. caused a slight flush to work its way from beneath the high points of Dalsany's starched white collar and up his neck. While he'd told his great-aunt of the codicil, he'd neglected to mention his massive debts, and he held his breath until the lady went on.

"But for all that Edgar was a good brother and a jolly good horseman. Too bad you look like those Pagets. I always said they were a bit too dangerous looking, but there's nothing to be done on that score. Is there?"

"No, your grace."

"Oh, come now, Dalsany, you must relax." A smile softened the ancient lines of the dowager duchess's face, and she winked in conspiratorial style as she pushed the serving dish of kippers toward him. The boy looked as if he didn't get enough to eat. "You did the right thing coming to me, young man. I'm not the dragon everyone claims, at least not when it involves a relative in need, and you're not to worry, for I'd love to help you. It shall be a treat, in fact, for I haven't faced a challenge like this in ages." She rested a bony finger against her jaw in a pondering sort of gesture, then stated, "I'll begin with a few pointed remarks to Almack's patronesses; two of them are my goddaughters. That alone would probably suffice, but I've another notion. Once we've let the ton know the Earl of Harrow's heir is in my good graces and looking for a bride, what do you say to a gala ball? I shall open Exeter House to Mayfair's *crème de la crème* and their eligible daughters.''

''I'd say, your grace, that it's a superlative notion and I'm exceedingly fortunate,'' he replied with sincere gratitude, for he knew that without this venerable lady's endorsement the chances of a gamester and rakehell such as himself reentering polite society were remote.

The plans for a ball had proceeded. Two hundred invitations edged in gold were issued, an orchestra was engaged, dinner and breakfast menus were decided upon, and hothouse flowers and orange trees were ordered from the Exeter country estate. Now, three weeks later, here Dalsany was at midnight slinking off to the terrace of Exeter House to smoke a cheroot.

Devil at bit, but he'd been introduced to more young ladies than he'd imagined populated the West End, and he'd signed his name to as many dance cards as was possible. There had been a gavotte with the exquisite redhead Lady Emmeline Duncombe, but she was frightfully dull-witted and quite incapable of stringing together enough words to compose a single sentence. There was a Scots reel with Lady Pamela Luttrell, who despite a dowry rumored to be in excess of a thousand pounds, was a dedicated blue-stocking with distinct notions of a husband's role in some bizarre matrimonial institution she termed a ''partnership of equals.'' After which there followed minuets and mazurkas and country dances with a score of other eligible females who were either penniless or bossy, unrelenting chatterboxes or horrendously hard on the eye.

Dalsany knew he couldn't afford to be persnickety, but he found it quite impossible to be otherwise. Marriage was an awe inspiring proposition, no matter how dire the alternative, and he had to make sure that the young lady he selected was at least capable of intelligent conversation, and at best didn't expect him to play the dutiful husband and rusticate with her and a brood of offspring.

He pulled a cheroot from his waistcoat pocket, struck a match on a granite balustrade, and leaned against the wall as he inhaled. He wasn't sure if he could survive many more nights such as this. Regardless of the codicil deadline, he'd better find a suitable girl before his toes were permanently maimed and his patience frayed beyond recovery.

From the ballroom, the lilting strains of a waltz drifted out to the terrace. It was the dinner dance, and the viscount smiled, knowing he'd wisely managed to keep this time free for a brief escape from the crush of partygoers. Again, he inhaled, enjoying the peace of the night, the rustle of the wind in the uppermost branches of a massive oak, and the muted rattle of carriage wheels from the other side of the garden wall. From somewhere in the garden a discordant noise caught his attention. It was a peculiar mewling, perhaps an injured cat, he speculated, glancing about for any sign of the creature. He peered beyond the terrace and into a bower of willow trees, where he espied a young lady seated on a wrought iron chair. The sound, he realized, was that of her crying.

Curious, he pushed away from the wall to walk

toward the bower, and moving closer, he recognized her. Earlier in the evening he'd caught sight of this particular young lady, abandoned to her own devices and sitting on a chair at the edge of the dance floor. Without qualification, she was the prettiest young lady in attendance; indeed, perhaps it was not farfetched to claim she was the loveliest female he'd ever seen.

Masses of soft golden curls tumbled about a cherubic heart-shaped face; she reminded him of a Botticelli angel with plump pink lips in a perfect little bow and creamy skin touched with a hint of shell pink along high cheekbones. *Exquisite* was the best word to describe her, and why such a perfect creature wasn't surrounded by a swarm of attentive gentlemen was most mysterious. If there was anyone to whom he'd truly wished an introduction this night, it was this young lady, but unlike the other ingenues in attendance, she had no aggressive mother by her side to effect such an introduction, and as for himself, he'd been so beset by parents pushing their marriageable daughters upon him that he'd been unable to make her acquaintance.

Now presented with a sterling opportunity, he was unaccountably ill at ease. It wasn't like the viscount not to know how to behave around the fairer sex, but then he didn't have a vast amount of experience with crying females, and he found the immediacy of her despair most unsettling. Clearly, the cause of her distress was more deeply rooted than a torn hem or crushed nosegay, and having discerned that bit of intelligence about a perfect stranger, he couldn't help feeling as if he was intruding on a private moment.

He tossed his cheroot aside and paused at the entrance to the bower, waiting to see if she had heard his footsteps and might stop crying, but instead of abating, her sobs seemed to grow in their intensity. Of a sudden, Dalsany was seized by the most inexplicable urge to do whatever was necessary to stop those tears.

Acting as he supposed a smitten swain might do, he entered the bower and fell to one knee by her side, whereupon the most astounding torrent of amorous words spewed forth from his lips.

"Hush, beautiful one, you mustn't carry on. Pray, what could one so lovely have to mourn? Surely, the future lies before you, and you merely need ask in order that the whole of it be yours."

A great sob caught in Lucy's throat, and she raised her head to stare at the gentleman kneeling before her. She hadn't heard anyone approach, and while his softly spoken words caught her by surprise, they were not half as unexpected as was the sight of the gentleman himself. Gazing upon the handsome young man with ink-black hair and strong masculine features, Lucy's heart somersaulted, and she gasped, then blinked and rubbed her teary eyes as if to correct her vision.

"Pip," she whispered in a voice so tiny Dalsany couldn't make sense of what she said. A tiny smile teased the corners of her mouth, and for one glorious heart-stopping moment she thought it was her old friend, but in the next instant she knew otherwise, and all vestige of that smile vanished.

"Are you all right, my lady?" Dalsany inquired. He observed the play of emotions across her countenance and was worried that she might again collapse into tears. "I didn't mean to frighten you."

His soft voice and sympathetic expression conveyed concern. Something about this gentleman touched a chord in Lucy, and she didn't hesitate in her response. "I'm fine now, sir. Thank you. It was merely that for an instant you reminded me of someone I used to know."

"And that drove you to tears?" he jested. Grinning in an irresistibly devilish manner, he added, "I've been accused of many regrettable acts, my lady, but never that."

Lucy couldn't help giggling. "Oh, you know I wasn't talking about *that*," she said while her thoughts focused on the actual source of her despair. Her expression became pensive.

"I know," was the gentleman's empathetic reply. He was serious, but his manner remained gentle. "Would you like to talk about it? Sometimes it helps to tell someone. And if not me, then perhaps a friend."

New tears welled in Lucy's eyes and she bit her lower lip to still its trembling. "That's the problem, you see. I haven't got a friend in the world. I did have one. Margaret. I'm staying with her family, but she's married and going to have a baby and her husband won't let her come to town. So I haven't got Margaret, nor her mother either, for the countess isn't at all like I remember." This guileless revelation spilled forth in a single breath.

Dalsany was intrigued by this forthright young lady. She was a novelty, and he wished to know more. "Tell me, how do you recall this countess?"

She commenced another ingenuous explanation: "Oh, full of warmth and understanding and infinitely patient no matter what. But, truth to tell, she's really quite horrid. She's the highest of high sticklers and a snob, and nothing I do pleases her. She said I was a hoyden for climbing the tree. But how else was I to rescue Mathilde? And then she told me that my ball gown''—Lucy's voice caught and she was forced to start over—''my ball gown was gauche and that I was no better than a trollop. I picked it out myself, you know, because the green matched my eyes, but I suppose that was not as clever as I thought.''

This girl a trollop? His assessing gaze took in the wounded expression upon her angelic face. She was as innocent and charming as she was lovely, and the viscount chuckled. ''Believe me, my lady, you must take the word of a man about town. You're not a trollop, and this countess is, indeed, prodigiously starched up to suggest such a thing.''

Once again a smile nudged Lucy's mouth upward. ''Thank you, sir.''

''Although I must say climbing trees—no matter how noble one's intention might be—is frowned upon by even the most libertine, and therefore is an activity that should be avoided. At least, while you're in Town,'' he amended in a friendly sort of aside, thinking that he rather liked the notion of a young lady who cared so little for convention that she would climb a tree and allow all the world to see.

His amiable words of caution caused the smile upon Lucy's face to broaden.

''Tell me, what else has this harridan said to upset you?'' he urged her to confide, firmly believing that anything the woman had said must have been grounded in jealousy and malice.

''Nothing more to me directly, but I overheard her talking with Lady Spencer in the ladies' retiring room.''

''And that's why you were crying?''

Frowning, she offered an affirmative nod.

"Was it really that dreadful?"

"Oh, yes, much worse than dreadful." Again, she launched into eager clarification. "The countess was complaining to Lady Spencer that she didn't know what she was going to do with me. She said I wasn't malleable and owned not a shred of shame. She called me an albatross and declared it didn't matter that Mr. Bradshaw had paid her an enormous sum to sponsor me because no amount of money was going to make up for my questionable parentage." She made a bleak gesture with her hands and turned away, fresh tears starting to her eyes. "Don't you see? The countess didn't agree to sponsor me because I was Lady Margaret's friend, she only did it because she was paid to. When I heard that it was the most lowering and most mortifying moment of my life. I'm sure everyone in all of Mayfair must know. Can you imagine what they're thinking of me? No wonder no one has asked me to dance. And while I suppose I shall eventually recover from the humiliation, I shan't recover if I fail."

"Fail?"

"In my ambition," she said wistfully. "Marrying and having babies. I know you probably think me dreadfully vulgar to speak of such things to a gentleman, but truly that's all I wish for in life."

Dalsany almost tumbled back on his haunches. Not only was she lovely, but she wanted to get married, not an altogether remarkable ambition; however, it *was* remarkable that this young lady wanted to be a mother. He'd always believed ladies feared childbirth and the subsequent damage to their health and waistlines, but apparently he was mistaken, or at least in this case. The dark specter of the codicil began to fade, and although the viscount's parting words to Mr. Frith had been spoken in jest, he could almost believe in the prospect of falling in love.

What remarkable good fortune. His search was over and his mind was made up. This was the young lady who would become his wife, his countess, and the mother of his requisite children. With that decision firmly made, he was seized by an unfamiliar sense of possessiveness which moved him to query, "Are you always this friendly with strangers?"

Lucy's cheeks flushed a bright shade of crimson. She whispered, "No."

"But I reminded you of someone," he said gently.

"Yes," was her shy reply.

Dalsany's heart contracted. She was a babe in the world. Vulnerable and innocent and filled with hopes, and he wasn't going to let those hopes be dashed. How serendipitous it was that they had met like this. He spoke in his most gallant manner. "I can't imagine why any sensible gentleman would consider your parentage an impediment to making and furthering your acquaintance."

"You can't?"

"Indeed, not. Aside from the fact that you're quite lovely, it's obvious you're educated and motivated by naught but high moral intent." He offered a grin that was at once warm and more than a little seductive. Rising from his knee to stand before her, he executed an elegant bow. "Allow me to introduce myself. I am Anthony Paget, Viscount Dalsany."

Twin dots of color highlighted Lucy's cheeks, and she angled her head to glance at him from beneath lowered eyelashes. "And I am Miss Lucy Wickham," she said, wishing that she might have been able to affix a grand title to her name.

"Well, Miss Wickham, it's an honor to make your acquaintance." He reached out and drew her gloved hand to his lips for the quickest and most circumspect of kisses. "And you would do me an even greater honor if you would permit me to call upon you and take you for a drive in the park tomorrow afternoon."

Her hand tingled from his touch, her heart was beating a furious tattoo, and Lucy found she required a few seconds before she could reply. "I should like that immensely, sir."

"Good, and you're smiling again. I like that. Now there's just one final thing we must do to remedy this evening."

"There is?" She was still rather breathless.

"Indeed." He extended an arm toward her and was heartened that she trusted him enough to put her hand in his and stand. "My dear Miss Wickham, you must not allow the night to end without dancing." The wonderment upon her sweet face made him smile, and pulling her into his arms, he declared, "And, my dear Miss Wickham, what a dance it shall be, for I believe the orchestra is playing a waltz."

Lucy laughed at his lighthearted tone and allowed the viscount to lead her in a waltz. Down the path they spun. Nothing the countess had said mattered anymore, and as they twirled in circles through the moonlit garden, Lucy was certain she had fallen madly in love.

Four

IT WAS A WHIRLWIND COURTSHIP and tongues wagged from day one.

Have you heard about Dalsany and the Wickham chit? the gabblemongers carried on behind gloved hands and raised ivory fans.

For two weeks in a row the viscount escorted Miss Wickham for a carriage ride every afternoon at the fashionable hour. On several occasions, they were observed enjoying petits fours and flavored ices at Gunter's beneath the sign of the pineapple on Berkeley Square, and one morning, the tattles gasped, Miss Wickham lost her bonnet as the couple galloped flat out across Hyde Park. It appeared, the tabbies hissed, they were a well-suited pair. Granted, she'd been schooled at the Royal Brighton, but that hardly made up for the fact that she was a female of unknown parentage and owned the most deplorable penchant for unseemly behavior. What proper young lady would dare to be seen sailing a miniature sailboat in the Serpentine? *On dit* the viscount had purchased the toy for Miss Wickham and had encouraged her interest in the miniature regatta, but then Dalsany was a gentleman whose reputation was already established as quite beyond the pale, and one could hardly expect any better from him.

Midway into the third week following the Exeter ball, their names appeared on several pages in the betting book at White's. The odds favored an early June betrothal, a May date was the long shot, and on the morning of May 23, the elderly Duke of Portland found himself two thousand pounds plumper in the pocket when a betrothal announcement was published in the *Times*. A few eyebrows were raised at the concluding statement—"At the Earl of Harrow's request the wedding ceremony shall take place at Clovelly Priory, Dorset"—and a few malicious whisperings circulated about the future groom's relationship with his uncle and his possible motivation for marrying, but then, as was the case with nine-day wonders, Miss Wickham and Viscount Dalsany were soon forgotten and the vicious eye of Society focused on another unsuspecting soul.

To honor the betrothed couple the dowager duchess gave an engagement fete, a proper affair to which some eighty of her closest friends had been invited. After receiving her guests in the marble rotunda of Exeter House, her grace announced the betrothal between Miss Wickham and Viscount Dalsany, and celebratory dancing with the happy couple forming the first set commenced.

"Do you mean we should leave straightaway for your uncle's home?" Lucy inquired as she took Dalsany's arm to move through the opening steps of a minuet.

The viscount held Lucy's hand in the air, and she circled to the right. He answered her question in a low voice. "I don't see why not. I know the wedding date is yet to be finalized, but I thought you'd like to meet what there is of my family and get to know Clovelly.'' As Lucy executed an elegant little turn and gracefully circled in the other direction, he mused to himself what a pleasure it was going to be to show her off in the neighborhood. No one in Dorset had ever thought he'd amount to much, not even his adoring baby sisters, and he was certain the earl had been most incredulous that he'd managed to find a willing bride. The sooner they went to Clovelly the better. He spoke for Lucy's ears only. ''My grandmother is in residence at the dower house along with my sisters, and you can stay with them, so you needn't worry about a chaperone. Besides, why would you wish to stay another day with Lord and Lady Mersham, if you had the choice?''

They cast a simultaneous glance toward the perimeter of the dance floor where a lady and gentleman were standing with the dowager countess. All three were smiling, each being exceedingly pleased with the recent turn of events. The dowager duchess, knowing full well the truth of Dalsany's financial distress, was satisfied that he'd found a young lady, albeit untitled, willing to be his wife. Lady Mersham was pleased to have divested herself of Miss Wickham with half the allotted housing allowance untouched, and her husband was vastly relieved that his wife would henceforth cease harping upon the tiresome burden she'd undertaken this Season. Now, God forbid, she could brag at her brilliance as a matchmaker in hopeless cases.

''You're right, of course. I should be thrilled to leave Mersham House,'' Lucy replied, trusting that she didn't sound ungrateful or like the sort of female who would take to managing one's husband's affairs. But how was she to explain to the viscount how strange it was to one moment have been consigned to a girls' boarding school, in the next dumped upon the London Season with a lady who resented her presence, and finally to find herself affianced and about to meet a family that would be hers? Far from ungrateful, she was in the throes of a dreadful insecurity. For the first time in many years, there was something precious in Lucy's life which she feared to lose. Forcing this apprehension to the back of her mind, she bestowed a shy smile upon the viscount and told only half the truth. "It's just that everything is happening so fast. I've hardly had time to adjust to any of it."

Dalsany's chest swelled with pride, and he returned her sweet smile. It was wonderful when Lucy gazed upon him like that, for she made him feel that he was someone important, and he liked that. Yes, he thought with satisfaction, marriage to Lucy was going to be a fine arrangement. He'd remain the Paget heir and secure the necessary funds to sustain his Town life, she'd get her family, and no doubt she'd come to adore life at Clovelly. It was an ideal setting to raise children, with its wide expanses of green lawn, a sea loch for boating and fishing, a plunge pool in a man-made grotto, and a spacious well-appointed nursery in the sunny south wing. An unexpected image of his uncle standing on the loggia and surveying his holdings caused the viscount to scowl.

"Is something wrong, Anthony?" asked Lucy as they began to repeat the short mincing pattern of the minuet.

The concern in her voice was touching, and he gave her hand a reassuring little squeeze. "I was merely wondering how to tell you about my uncle."

"Oh? He's not a terrible high stickler is he?"
Her green eyes widened. Those anxieties bubbled
anew, and wondering what might happen if the
earl didn't deem her good enough to marry his
nephew and heir, she gave voice to the dreaded
query, "He won't disapprove of me, will he?"

"Oh, no, dear girl, not that. He'll adore you as
surely as Grandmother and my sisters shall. And
everyone else in the neighborhood, for that matter. It's just that he isn't the warmest of souls,
and you mustn't expect a grand welcome. He was
wounded on the Peninsula, y'know, and I don't
think he's ever recovered from that. Mentally, I
mean. When he was forced to give up his command he retired to the country and made me his
heir. Rather soured him on socializing."

"What a tragic story," she said sadly. Tiny
frown lines marked her forehead.

Having never owned a single sympathetic consideration for his uncle, the viscount was startled
by Lucy's reaction. "Well, yes, I suppose it is."

"And now I understand why it is your uncle
wished us to go to Clovelly for the wedding. Well,
you needn't fear on my account, Anthony. I
promise I shan't do anything to offend him."
Only too well did Lucy understand the pain of
loneliness, and this insight prompted her to suggest, "Perhaps we might even draw him out of
his shell."

Dalsany's face became distinctly pinched in his
effort to conceal his cynical amusement. Draw the
earl out of his shell? he mused rhetorically. Not
likely, he chuckled, as he executed a deep bow to
Lucy's elegant curtsy. The stately dance was almost over.

"You're very generous, Lucy, to make such a
suggestion," he said, secure in the knowledge

that he'd found the perfect wife. She was kind and gentle-hearted, and although she was still quite young in many ways, he knew that in the years ahead she would be a loyal and devoted wife; the fact that she was beautiful was an added bonus. For a moment, a frisson of guilt niggled at his conscience, and he wondered if he should tell her about the codicil, but in the next instant, he thought better of it. He'd found a wife, and there was no sense in jeopardizing matters. It wasn't a good idea for Lucy to know too much about his less than respectable habits, nor did he wish her to know why it was that he was marrying. Of course, he liked and admired her, but the truth was he would never consider matrimony if it wasn't for the codicil, and since he cared deeply for Lucy's sensibilities, there was no point in telling her something that was bound to generate unhappiness. His thoughts returned to his uncle. "Just don't let him know you're feeling sorry for him or allow him to see you staring at him."

"Stare at him? Why should I do that?"

"His injuries," he supplied, somewhat astonished that Lucy hadn't heard about his uncle. He thought everyone knew about the valiant Earl of Harrow. Defeat at Albuera had been averted only by the steadfastness of the British troops, and it was the Royal Fusiliers that drove the French from the field. Not, however, without significant loss. Of the seven thousand British less than eighteen hundred men had been left standing, and the Earl of Harrow was the only officer to survive. "He lost an eye and wears a patch, and he nearly lost a leg. Grandmother says it was a miracle the surgeon didn't hack it off, but he swears it was no miracle, rather a curse and that he'd be better off without it. Sometimes the weather troubles him terribly, makes it so stiff with pain he can't even walk down to the dining room. Can't ride either, and that for a former officer and former master of the hounds is most distressing.''

The orchestra played the final notes of the minuet, and as Lucy and the viscount strolled off the dance floor to rejoin the dowager duchess, the girl's tender heart swelled with concern for the Earl of Harrow. Her every maternal instinct was aroused. Not only was she going to have a family, but apparently at least one member of that family needed her as much as she needed him.

Six days later the Paget family traveling coach— a freshly painted gold-and-scarlet coat of arms emblazoned upon the door—wheeled off the treeless Dorchester to Lyme Regis Road and down a drive lined by newly leafed oaks whose uppermost branches entwined overhead to form an archway beneath which all visitors to Clovelly Priory were required to enter. The drive wound through meticulous parkland, past a variety of follies and temples and alabaster statuary in glens landscaped with an artful profusion of spring flowers. Bright purple aubretia mingled with blankets of daffodils and crimson Holland tulips.

The whole of the journey had been curious owing to the omnipresence of soldiers and sailors and every manner of military transport clogging the byways 'round Southampton, and to the richness of the scenery through the New Forest and across the chalk, but never so curious as the grounds of this estate. Three centuries of meticulous landscaping had turned this stretch of barren coastline to a lush paradise—there were even several clusters of palm trees, the likes of which Lucy had theretofore only seen in picture books.

She inched forward on the velvet squabs for a better view of her new home.

The carriage rounded the next curve, and she was rewarded with a spectacular vista down a great ride to an enormous house that appeared to stand at the edge of the earth, for the tended grass stretched beyond the house to meet the southern horizon and fall to the sea below. Clovelly Priory itself was a structure of classical perfection in pale pink stucco, and the mid-afternoon sunshine glimmering off rows of Palladian windows lent to its magical appearance. With a massive horseshoe staircase of dark mauve brickwork being the focal point of the uniquely designed entrance to the house, Clovelly resembled Lucy's notion of a fairy-tale palace.

"Oh, it's lovely, Anthony. Positively lovely." She inhaled the salty air. From the distance, there was the unmistakable echo of waves tumbling upon the shore, and Lucy couldn't help feeling that she'd come home. "I must confess to having harbored trepidations about what to expect. As a rule a priory does conjure up images of gray toppling-down edifices, and after you told me about your uncle I began to expect an awfully dreary place."

"Ah, but that's not Clovelly. Not at all, and that's why I didn't tell you. Watching the surprise when someone sees Clovelly for the first time is a treat of which I shall never tire." The road swooped downward, the vehicle began the final approach to the house, and as Lucy tilted her head from side to side to catch every detail of the fabulous surroundings, the viscount went on. "There is, of course, legitimate reason for the name. Once upon a time it was a house of prayer. A relic of the Crusades, to be precise. It was a preceptory for sisters of the Order of the Knights Hospitallers until the earls of Harrow took residence and it became somewhat of an Elizabethan palace, but little trace of either of those structures remains. In the last century, my great-grandfather, the eighth earl, commenced a series of renovations and embellishments under the guidance of the Scotsman Robert Adam.''

''What a lot you know about it,'' Lucy remarked. The carriage reached level ground. Two leggy wolfhounds appeared from the nearby gardens to race the vehicle those final yards.

''I've always loved Clovelly,'' he stated with a notable measure of pride.

She responded with an understanding nod. ''Being named your uncle's heir must have been very special to you, indeed.''

This remark had the unforeseen effect of causing Dalsany to blush, and in the hopes Lucy wouldn't notice his sudden discomposure he called out to the wolfhounds, ''Hallo, Arthur. Hallo, Cnut.'' Verily, he loved Clovelly, the house and surrounding lands, but that fondness wasn't the reason why becoming the eleventh Earl of Harrow was so important, and he knew this was his chance to tell the truth about the codicil. But he didn't breathe a word of any of it to Lucy, and when she exclaimed, ''Oh, Anthony, I love it already, and I do believe I shall adore living here,'' he vowed that she would never know the truth from his lips.

The traveling coach came to a stop at the foot of the horseshoe staircase, whereupon Lucy popped her head out the window and caught sight of a tall lady in maroon silk, several strands of pearls about her neck, and her silver hair swept away from a refined face into a chignon. At seventy-one, the Dowager Countess of Harrow was as imposing as she'd been at twenty-two, when the statuesque Scots beauty had left the Highlands to wed her third cousin.

In the informal tradition of the Highlands, the dowager countess preferred to be called Lady Bronwen, and her natural poise and unpretentious ways were remarkable. As a young bride she'd won the favor and respect of half the populace of Dorset. Now, as the dowager she was the Paget matriarch and the most respected lady in the county.

On either side of Lady Bronwen stood two young ladies wearing the sort of woolen pinafores made especially for schoolgirls. They were the viscount's fifteen-year-old twin sisters, with identical winged brows above slanting eyes, high cheekbones, and narrow aristocratic noses. But their hair coloring, and therefore their initial impression upon a stranger, was not at all alike: Lady Edith was a redhead as her grandmother had once been, while Lady Eglantine had gypsy-black hair. The girls were giggling and waving, and Lucy was about to return their effusive greeting when she noticed the gentleman standing on the step above the trio of Paget females.

Lucy regarded him in stunned amazement. He was extremely tall and dark of hair and complexion, a black patch covered one eye, and he was leaning heavily upon a cane. Lean thighs were encased in skintight nankeen breeches, and he wore highly polished boots to the knees. His shirt and simple cravat were crisp and white in contrast to skin bronzed by the elements, and the muscles of his broad shoulders were outlined by an expertly tailored navy jacket. He was hatless, and that dark hair, black as a moonless night and streaked with a touch of silver at the temples, was longer than was the current fashion and slightly unruly as it fell over the jacket collar.

The Earl of Harrow, a forbidding scowl etched upon his features, had never looked more like a pirate than he did at that precise moment. A prickling of gooseflesh spread over Lucy's entire body, followed by an odd inward tremor. Quickly, she looked over her shoulder at Dalsany, then to the tall gentleman leaning on the cane and again back to Dalsany. With stunning clarity she knew why her fiancé's ink-black hair and deep blue eyes had been familiar. The gentleman standing on the horseshoe steps was her Pip, and Lucy's heart skipped a beat.

In all the time that had passed since that last August on their special beach, she'd never forgotten Pip. At first, she'd remembered him with anger, and she'd cried herself to sleep, night after night, wondering why he hadn't said farewell as he'd done before; then she had remembered him with the adolescent pain of unrequited love, and she'd cried every day for a week when Lady Anne had appeared the next August accompanied by a gentleman other than Pip. Lucy had worked up the courage to pay a call upon Battersea Hall and she'd written a little speech, but Lady Anne had refused to receive her and the speech had been tossed into the waves, leaving Lucy to rely upon her imagination to supply whatever explanations she might.

He'd been beset by a band of highwaymen, she fancied, and died in a ditch on Hounslow Heath, or mayhap had lost his memory. Perhaps, she imagined, he'd met a beautiful girl at Almack's. Of course, they had married and were living in matrimonial bliss on his family estate surrounded by a brood of healthy pink-cheeked children. She didn't like to think of him being dead, but that was vastly more comforting than having to come to terms with the fact that he'd left without a word, a fact that spoke volumes as to how little their relationship had meant to him.

That was the deepest wound of all. For Lucy, her friendship with Pip had been the most important bond with another human beyond the academy walls, and to think that Pip could go off without giving her a second thought was intolerable.

In the end, however, it was the joy of those summers that remained brightest upon her mind's eye. Verily, it was Pip's memory that had sustained Lucy when her classmates had graduated and she had remained behind, neither student nor teacher, in the cottage in the cherry orchard. Whenever she caught herself feeling sorry for herself, Lucy would recall those three glorious summers. She knew most people never enjoyed a friendship such as she had known, and in that sense she had already lived a lifetime and her heart was full. And so she dreamed and clung to a memory, and somewhere deep in her heart she had always yearned for this moment when they would be reunited.

Her lips moved to call out his name, her hand clutched the door handle, and she edged forward on the seat preparatory to jumping down. Then her hand fell away and her mouth closed before she'd uttered a peep. Although it was her initial reaction to call out to Pip and to burst forth from the carriage and into his familiar embrace, his forbidding demeanor caused her to sink back against the carriage squabs in quiet confusion.

"What's wrong, my darling?" Dalsany saw dismay and bewilderment mix upon Lucy's face. The color had disappeared from her cheeks. She looked positively lost, and he clasped her right hand in his, then dropped a reassuring kiss upon her cheek. "I know he looks ferocious but don't fret, I promise they shall all adore you. Even my uncle."

"They're here at last," Lady Bronwen, as was her habit, stated the obvious.

"Indeed," the earl drawled, leaning upon the cane to descend and stand at her side.

"Oh, don't sound like such a doubting Thomas," she scolded her eldest and only surviving offspring. Over the years, her Highland brogue had gentled; rarely did she employ the quaint colloquialisms she had spoken as a girl in the Highlands, and only when she was vexed, as she was at this moment, did the brogue return. "Enow, Alex, you set the rules, and Dalsany's complied. Truth to tell, I'm really rather proud of Anthony. Don't you agree? I never thought the boy had it in him."

The earl give a derisive snort. His mother, usually the shrewdest of females, owned the most deplorable weak spot for Dalsany. "Wouldn't put it past him to have hired some Covent Garden bit of muslin to play the part for my benefit. I've never heard of a Wickham family."

"Oh, Alex, hush, do be quiet. They're getting out now. Look, she's younger than I supposed, very pretty and very sweet." Again she stated the obvious. "And by the looks of it she's terrified. Poor child. Behave yourself, Alex, and don't do anything to frighten the gel off," she ordered in her most imperious tone as she pinched his forearm for parental emphasis before gliding down the steps with arms extended to embrace her grandson and his fiancée.

The last of the estate staff hurried to their places on the drive. Gardeners, grooms, and gillies formed a queue to the left, and the majordomo and household staff stood to the right while the ladies Edith and Eglantine bounced about the carriage, causing their governess to roll her eyes heavenward. Several Jack Russells yapped at the wolfhounds, a quartet of porters in scarlet livery rushed forward to retrieve the mountain of luggage, and no one noticed the stupefaction etched upon the earl's face. His lordship froze on the mauve staircase, one hand gripping the ivory handle of his cane and a muscle in his jaw twitching as he observed the young woman who had just stepped down from the traveling coach.

He noticed first the expensive fabric of her China blue traveling costume and he knew Dalsany could not have afforded to outfit her in such style. This was no charade, he surmised, speculating in the next second that Miss Wickham might be an heiress and thus his wily nephew could claim triumph on two fronts. He watched the young woman as her slender gloved hand pressed against a gold locket at the base of her throat. It was an open and vulnerable gesture, causing the earl to conclude that Miss Wickham was exceedingly inexperienced. He scrutinized her. It appeared she was a blonde. Several strands of pale gold hair had fallen from beneath her blue satin bonnet. And she was tall, nearly as tall as Dalsany, a bit too tall for his taste, he amended this silent appraisal, but shapely, nonetheless. Then the oddest notion hit him.

Sweet heaven, he knew her, but from where he

could not precisely recall, and he searched his memory like the pages of a textbook, yet he could not fathom how he might know her. He watched as she commenced talking to one of the twins, the wide brim of her bonnet blocking her face from his view, but her head moved from side to side, indicative of an animated conversation, and her hands rose and fluttered like sparrows when a farmer's wife scatters parsley seed.

The twins were smiling at something she said, a ripple of girlish laughter rose between them, and in that instant, the earl knew. He remembered those hot summer days, the fishing and picnics and sailing expeditions and the pervasive aura she had created that there was naught but good in the world. He remembered it all, especially the promise of exquisite beauty, and he knew without seeing that her mouth in repose formed a perfect bow and that her eyes were a dazzling lush green like the English hillsides in spring.

The commotion of the present faded away, and instead the earl heard waves crashing and the light melody of innocent laughter drifting on a summer wind. He closed his eyes, hardly aware that he was standing on the steps of Clovelly, and he listened to her dulcet voice: *I think I'd like to marry you, sir.* He exhaled a pent-up breath and opened his eyes to see that promise of beauty fulfilled.

She was clinging to Dalsany as if her very life depended upon him, and fierce emotions tore through the earl. First, there was a sort of blinding joy that at least one decent remnant of his past had survived, then there was deep anger mixed with jealousy. He recalled his own less than proper thoughts and those emotions deepened.

No one, no gentleman regardless of rank or accomplishment, let alone his blackguard nephew Dalsany, would ever deserve a young lady as special as his Minx.

Five

T HE BEDCHAMBER WAS EXQUISITE, all floral
chintz in cornflower blue accented by a touch
of violet. The walls were pale gold with plaster
medallions in the style of Robert Adam above the
fireplace and doorways, and there was a massive
oriel window that looked out over the sweep of
lawns to the whitecaps of the English Channel
beyond. Sunshine filled the room, and as etiquette dictated, fresh flowers graced the marble
mantel and the round table beside the canopied
bed, but Lucy didn't notice any of this.

Her head was pounding as she paced the floor
wondering how she had managed to survive
those moments on the horseshoe staircase when
she had been introduced to Pip. No, she corrected
herself, he wasn't Pip anymore, he was the Earl
of Harrow.

"Miss Wickham, welcome to Clovelly Priory,"
the earl had said in a low voice devoid of any
emotion. That there had been no smile, nor
warmth, in his expression had pierced Lucy's
heart nearly to breaking, and the worst of it was
he hadn't even shown the slightest flicker of recognition for her.

That was all he'd said. Nothing more. Then

he'd made a proper excuse, given a curt bow, and had gone off to meet with his estate manager. But what was she to expect? Clearly, he didn't have the vaguest notion who she was. After all, he could hardly be expected to recognize her after so many years, she consoled herself. The Earl of Harrow was a man of much experience, and there was no earthly reason why such a gentleman would ever have held two thoughts for a truant schoolgirl with bare feet and sand clinging to her hair.

She pressed her fingers to her temple. It wasn't supposed to be happening like this. Her arrival at Clovelly Priory was supposed to herald the beginning of a future in which security and happiness were guaranteed. She bit her lower lip to still its trembling and entertained the wholly ironic thought that she wished she'd never left her cottage in the cherry orchard at the academy. At least there the future, albeit barren, had been predictable. At least there she had been able to hold on to the best of her memories and cherish the secret fantasy of an idyllic reunion with Pip.

The bedchamber door opened, drawing Lucy from her troublesome reverie. She turned as a maid entered carrying a tea tray, and directly behind her came the twins, Lady Edith and Lady Eglantine.

"Oh, hallo," said Lucy, determining in that moment that she must make every effort to conceal her disquietude. She must proceed as if nothing were out of the ordinary, and most of all, she must not let anyone know she had ever met the earl, for if he didn't recall her, she could hardly be the one to broach the subject. It would be terribly bad ton to embarrass one's host and an even more terrible way to start off with her new family.

"You don't mind if we come in, do you?" asked the dark-haired Eglantine. She hovered a few inches inside the doorway while Edith had already proceeded to the settee by the window, plopped herself on the blue velvet cushions, and helped herself to a triangle of shortbread from the tea tray.

Lucy smiled. "Not at all. I've already changed from my traveling costume and would love some company. Do come in."

"Thank you." Eglantine came closer and returned Lucy's smile, then she said to her twin, "The dinner gong shall ring soon, and you know Grandmother will be furious if you ruin your appetite."

Edith stared daggers at her sister and took another buttery triangle.

"I'm sure a little tea won't hurt," Lucy intervened. "I'm famished after the journey and quite in need of a little something to tide me over." She hooked her arm through Eglantine's and led her to the settee, where they joined the redhead. Having poured three cups of tea, Lucy asked Eglantine, "Won't you have just one small piece of shortbread? It looks delicious, and I'm sure it won't hurt."

"Thank you anyway, and you're quite right." She sat upright, hands folded in her lap, legs crossed at the ankles, every bit the model of a very proper young lady. "It likely wouldn't do anything to ruin my appetite, but it might wreak havoc upon my complexion. All that butter, y'know," she said in a lofty tone of voice, affecting the world-weary manner of a sophisticated and very grand lady.

Edith, who was lounging more than sitting, rolled her eyes toward the ceiling, and Lucy repressed a giggle. These twins were as different as night was from day.

Making a stab at conversation, Lucy remarked, "I was rather surprised when the housekeeper brought me to this room. I thought I would be staying in the dower house."

"We've all moved back into Clovelly," supplied Edith. She dusted shortbread crumbs off her skirt and went on. "We'd all have been horrendously under one another's feet at the dower house, besides which, Grandmother said that if Clovelly was to be your home, you should get to know it right away."

Eglantine set down her teacup and gave a wistful little sigh. "She also said it was high time that Uncle Alex had company."

"And that he learned once again to sit at the table with other people like a civilized soul ought to," quipped Edith in a manner than made Lucy suspect she was parroting the dowager countess.

While a stranger might have considered this exchange somewhat humorous, Lucy found it sobering. In her mind's eye, she saw Pip laughing, his eyes dancing with merriment as he dared her to dash headlong into the surf. Then she saw the earl as he had been this afternoon, leaning upon the cane, his expression dour, and one of those glorious blue eyes hidden forever behind a black patch. Something inside Lucy twisted, and she required several moments before she could inquire, "Your uncle is a recluse?"

"Of late." This brief remark came from Edith, who seemed more intent on hoarding shortbread in her pinafore pockets than providing Lucy with an informative response.

Eglantine was more forthcoming. "When we were children he was hardly here at all. Of course, there was his commission in the Royal Fusiliers and the war on the Peninsula which kept him away from us, but before that he was quite a man about town, and it if wasn't the Season in Mayfair that filled his diary, he was off at one country house or another. He was an excellent horseman, forever receiving mention in the newspapers. I've oodles of clippings, even from the *Times*. He was master of the hounds, y'know, and always riding one hunt or another. And in constant demand with the ladies. Grandmother said more than one conspiring miss contrived to catch him in a parson's mousetrap, and it was a miracle he escaped their ploys. He was very eligible, you see. Oh, if only you could have known him then." She heaved another sigh worthy of Drury Lane. "And now he has nothing."

The sting of tears burned Lucy's nose and she shut her eyes, wondering how she would ever keep the past a secret when it seemed as if her heart was going to break with sadness for her old friend's pain. She recalled her conversation with the viscount and her suggestion that she coax his uncle out of his shell. Verily, she wished to find Pip and tell him the cane and the eye patch didn't matter one jot and now that she was here he wouldn't be alone anymore, but Lucy knew that wasn't possible. All she said was, "I'm sorry, so very sorry."

"So are Edith and Grandmother and I, and Anthony, too, I suppose, but you mustn't let Uncle Alex know. None of us do. Not ever."

"He's got the most horrendous temper, you see," was Edith's sober explanation, said in such a tenor that it sounded as if she were divulging the most frightful confidence.

Out of the blue, Eglantine changed the subject.

"Have you and Anthony made your wedding plans yet?"

"Not really," replied Lucy. The tea was starting to have a calming effect upon her, and she was beginning to feel more like herself.

"Oh, if I were you, I should have already selected the flowers. Budding gardenias and yellow sweetbrier roses. And the cake. At least four tiers with yellow-tinted icing and sugar leaves in green. And, of course, the music. It would be Mozart or Bach. Something very dramatic with brass accompaniment. Perhaps I could help you with the music selection."

"Oh, do hush up, Eglantine. She only wants to help because she's leagues in love with the organist at the chapel in Fleet Regis. Mr. Pratt's his name, Jonathan Horatio Pratt, and he's the most dreadful gossip and always asking the sort of questions no one else would dare broach. Grandmother's says he's a boor, and she'd be positively livid if she knew you'd written him a poem."

"Edith! How could you?" Eglantine blushed, then paled. "Oh, you won't tell anyone, will you, Miss Wickham?"

"Of course, I shan't, and you mustn't call me Miss Wickham. We're soon to be relatives, almost sisters. You must call me Lucy or else I shall feel like a guest and a veritably ancient one at that."

"Oh, we wouldn't want you to feel like a guest, nor ancient," said Edith, and the girls agreed to call her Lucy, after which Eglantine announced, "Grandmother is planning a gala ball, you know, although Uncle Alex says he won't attend."

"Well, what would you expect?" demanded Edith in exasperation. "Honestly, Eglantine, you're just too romantic for your own good. You must learn to be more sensible. Think about it.

Uncle Alex can hardly dance, so why would he wish to attend a party?''

Eglantine appeared deflated. "And why not? He's ever so mysterious and handsome. Don't you think so, Lucy?''

Lucy's face warmed and her palms turned moist. "Well, yes, he is," came her admission, and her heart did an odd little flip-flop as she pictured him standing on the horseshoe staircase that afternoon.

"You see, Edith, even Lucy agrees." There was a triumphant note of vindication in Eglantine's pronouncement. "And I'm sure oodles of girls would love to dance with Uncle Alex. Cane and eye patch and all.''

"Well, no matter what you think, he still won't be there. Mark my words. Nothing could force Uncle Alex to show up at a ball, not even a command from Grandmother.''

From the depths of the house the dinner bell sounded. Edith jumped to her feet and headed toward the corridor. Eglantine rose more sedately and took hold of Lucy's right hand.

"I'm so very glad you're here, Lucy, and that you're going to marry Anthony." She lowered her voice to confide, "Edith would laugh at me if she ever knew, but at night I always say a little prayer that Anthony and Uncle Alex will each find someone as pretty and nice as you, and at last, one of my prayers has been answered.''

Lucy made some appropriate remark, bland, yet polite, and as they walked down the corridor, she paid undue attention to the tips of her toes. Eglantine's remark had had the unfortunate effect of bringing fresh tears to her eyes. Only half of the girl's prayer had been answered. Her brother was to finally find happiness, but what about the earl? Would he ever find someone with whom to share his life? Tears tickled her nose and she blinked in rapid succession. How could she rejoice in her betrothal? How could she and the viscount enjoy their gala celebration? It was no wonder the earl would not attend the ball when their future was in some ways to be at the expense of his.

"Would you like a tour of the house on the way down?" asked Eglantine.

"Yes, if you please," Lucy replied, eager for the time to compose herself.

They ambled down the length of a gallery past time-darkened portraits of previous generations of Pagets. There were Cavaliers in Vandyke lace collars, their plumed hats tucked beneath an arm, their jeweled swords hanging at one side; there were gentlemen in long coats of flowered silk and brocade, wearing curling periwigs; there were ladies in elaborate court dress, and ladies seated in pastoral settings surrounded by children and family pets. A painting of a mother and her three children caught Lucy's attention. The mother was young, not more than twenty-two or twenty-three at the most, an infant was resting in the cradle of her arms, and standing on either side of the wrought iron bench were two young boys, one still so young he wore a damask linen dress, the other in a blue silk suit with white leggings, his hair in a queue, and perched upon his shoulder a tiny monkey. Contrary to the usual style of depicting sober expressions upon portrait subjects, this painting portrayed everyone, including the infant, smiling, and Lucy's heart contracted with longing.

Nothing had changed. She still desired a family, and she still intended to uphold the solemn

vow to her mother's memory as well as the betrothal pledge she'd made to the viscount.

Of a sudden, Lucy experienced a flush of
shame. That she hadn't given one thought to her
fiancé since arriving at Clovelly Priory was dis-
graceful. The viscount was kind and thoughtful
and solicitous, and she should be thinking about
him, not worrying in excess about his uncle and
her childish memories. After all, the viscount was
the gentleman who had proposed to her and
would be her husband. In fact, she asked herself
as Eglantine led the way into an elegant oak-
paneled library, what more could she wish for in
a husband?

Six

HIS LIMP WASN'T TERRIBLY NOTICEABLE any longer. The earl knew that. Only on those days when a mist rolled in from the Channel or rains slashed across the downs did his leg stiffen and prevent him from getting about with ease. His recovery was progressing, slowly to be sure, but it was progressing, and of late he'd begun to harbor the hope that come autumn he might be able to ride with the hunt once again. Nonetheless, on this particular evening he fell back upon a habit he'd adopted when he'd first returned from the Peninsula: a good five minutes before the dinner bell sounded the earl entered the dining room to wait for the others to arrive.

It was cowardly of him not to gather with the rest of the family in the library as was customary when his mother dined at Clovelly, and had his conduct been challenged, he wouldn't have denied it was less than gentlemanly as well as craven. But he'd had a shock this afternoon and needed these final private moments to compose himself before seeing *her* again.

Threading a hand through his thick hair, he considered those moments on the steps this afternoon when they'd been introduced. If only she'd

59

offered the slightest hint of recognition, he would
have behaved with far less formality. Instead,
he'd been forced to the distasteful role of acting
as if they were meeting for the first time. He'd
never forget her uncertain smile when she shook
his hand, nor the dismay upon her features as she
tried to ignore his black patch and cane. That she
hadn't recognized him was quite bad enough, but
the fact that the sight of him distressed her produced a far more profound jolt to his confidence.
He'd thought himself immune to the reaction of
others when they first regarded him, but apparently that wasn't true when it came to Lucy
Wickham and that was an altogether troubling
development to consider. Never before had the
earl found himself so discomposed by a female,
hence he'd offered a hasty excuse and retreated
to collect his thoughts.

Miss Wickham. Lucy Wickham. A small sun-
flushed face encircled by wet curls rose before his
mind's eye, and the frown lines about his eyes
and mouth relaxed. Finally, after all these years,
he had a name to match with the memory. Lucy.
It suited her. Light and sweet and not in the least
bit artificial.

He closed his eyes, remembering at once those
carefree August days and those hopeless weeks
in the hospital tent after Albuera. These two dis-
parate chapters in his life had become as one, for
in those lonely interminable hours on the Peninsula when there had been no one save the dead
and dying to hear his cries of agony, it had been
those summers on the beach below Battersea Hall
with his minx that had seen him through the end-
less nights.

Nothing, not even the memory of his parents,
nor the importance of surviving for the posterity

of the Paget line, had been as strong and vibrant a motivation as that vision of one young girl, whose fearless nature and eagerness to enjoy the world to its fullest had been a spark of hope to his dying heart. She had become his lifeline, and for that he owed her an immense debt, certainly, something better than being the one responsible for a marriage of convenience to Dalsany. In fact, he wondered with mounting trepidation, had Dalsany even told her of the codicil? Surely, she wasn't of the belief that his nephew had actually fallen in love.

A footman carrying an ebony mallet crossed the dining room, and the earl's glance followed the manservant toward the threshold, where he struck a Chinese gong four times. The others would soon arrive. The earl leaned heavily on the table as he stood to await them.

Footsteps echoed in the corridor. Muffled voices grew louder, and he heard laughter, one particularly light melody of amusement rising above the rest. How sweet and musical it was, and touched with a hint of playfulness. It was the laugh of a minx, he thought, as an unfamiliar pain knotted within his chest. Thank God she hadn't recognized him, for then he would surely have had to witness her pity and that would have been intolerable.

The first to enter were the twins.

"Oh, Uncle Alex, it's so exciting. We're all in the dining room at Clovelly once again with you at the head of the table. Just the way it should be." Eglantine stopped beside the earl to drop an affectionate kiss upon his jaw. "And we're about to have a new sister. It's almost too good to be true. Lucy's a prodigiously wonderful girl, y'know."

Offering a nod of accord, Edith promptly picked up where her sister had left off. "And ever so friendly. She wasn't in the least bit snobbish when we showed up at her room and helped ourselves to tea."

"Just wait 'til you get to know her, Uncle Alex. You're going to love her."

The earl snuffed out the girls' enthusiasm with a glower. Eglantine opened her mouth as if to challenge his dark expression, but the entrance of the rest of the dinner party distracted her. She glanced toward the doorway and the earl's gaze followed to fix on Lucy as she entered two steps behind Dalsany, who had his grandmother upon his arm.

Sweet heaven, Lucy was lovely. Young and pure and radiating hope. The earl swallowed hard as his gaze moved from a cherubic face framed by soft golden curls to an enticing female form. It was a potent combination. An innocent face above a figure which Venus would have envied. She was wearing a gown of sage-green China crepe with a high waistline and cinched bodice that accentuated firm round breasts. The tapered sleeves began at her shoulders to reveal a creamy expanse of neckline that made a man imagine what it would be like to touch that tiny hollow spot at the base of her throat. Again, he swallowed hard, and forced his gaze to move toward his mother as she took her seat at the opposite end of the table.

Lucy shivered. Although the earl was acting as if hadn't been watching her, she knew he had, and she also knew that Eglantine was right. He was the most devastatingly handsome man she'd ever seen, eye patch and all, and dressed in formal black, the royal blue of his iridescent waistcoat buttons matching the vibrant hue of his brooding gaze; he was undeniably masculine. Everything about his appearance—even the streaks of gray at the temples—added to this impression of male strength. Lucy's heart beat faster, and momentarily, she lowered her eyes and held her breath. She hadn't anticipated being seated beside the earl, and fearing to reveal her inner turmoil, she focused on a distant point beyond his shoulder before exhaling to address him in a voice that was barely above a whisper.

"Good evening, my lord."

The earl searched his brain for an appropriate nicety and managed to inquire, "You are rested from your journey, Miss Wickham?"

The use of her surname threatened to shatter Lucy's fragile composure. It served as a cruel reminder that Pip had not remembered his minx, and a nervous smile played upon her features. Praying that her lips weren't trembling too noticeably, she unfolded her serviette and replied in a stilted voice, "Yes, my lord, I am rested. Thank you."

He gave a silent nod. The heaviness in his chest had once again become painful as he observed the way she managed to avoid eye contact with him. The earl's jaw tightened with anger, for he knew it had been a mistake to dine with the others, a mistake to think that a stranger, particularly an innocent young girl, would accept him as he now was.

"You must tell us all about your Season, Lucy dear, and you must not omit a single detail," began Lady Bronwen. Unable to ignore the peculiar expression upon her son's countenance, she affected an overly animated tenor to mask her uneasiness. She knew Alex, in his stoicism, had cut himself off from society, assuming a hard and uncaring attitude. But this evening there was something different. This evening, there was an almost vulnerable edge to his manner, and her heart ached as it had when he'd first been brought home. He was a grown man, but he was still her child, and above all else Lady Bronwen wanted his happiness. And right now he should have been quite pleased with himself. Alex was getting what he wanted: the burden of marrying for the Paget line would soon be lifted from his shoulders and he could retreat into deeper seclusion from society. Why then did she detect this wholly uncharacteristic anxiety about him? And why did she get the impression, her shrewd Scots mind speculated, that Miss Lucy Wickham was the reason for his discomposure?

Determined to set a convivial mood, Lady Bronwen went on, "I haven't been to Town in several years and would enjoy your observations, Lucy." She paused to nod toward the major-domo, who in turn nodded toward the head footman, and as if by magic an invisible door in the wall opened and a line of servants entered carrying serving platters. As gold-rimmed bowls of lobster bisque were set before the diners, Lady Bronwen said, "How I recall my first glimpse of Mayfair. I was a young girl from north of Inverness, raised for a life of duty in my small corner of the Highlands, and I had seen nothing of the world. It quite bedazzled me."

"Oh, yes, every detail, if you please," begged Eglantine, who was a voracious reader of the socials column and clipped every reference to Beau Brummel for her collection. "Did you have a voucher for Almack's?"

"And were you allowed to waltz?" A touch of

scandal laced Edith's query, for the risqué dance had only been sanctioned by Almack's patronesses this Season.

"And did you attract Prinny's notice?" In her excitement, Eglantine did not see her grandmother's disapproval at her use of this vulgar reference to the Regent.

"It really wasn't all that spectacular," Lucy replied to this volley from the twins. Unused to being the center of attention, a shell pink flush spread across her cheeks, lending an almost magical aura to her simple presentation. "I was sponsored by the mother of an old school friend. And yes, I did have a voucher, although Almack's wasn't quite as dazzling as I'd imagined it would be. The cakes were stale and the punch rather watery. And as for the Regent, well, once I'd met Anthony no other gentleman dared approach me."

The twins made appropriate remarks, the viscount grinned at his singular role in this dissertation, and Lady Bronwen glanced toward her son. To her disappointment, the earl was scowling even worse than before.

"Tell us, Miss Wickham, how *did* you meet Anthony?" inquired the earl in a rather oversharp tenor. His narrow glance moved from Dalsany to Lucy and back once again to Dalsany.

The viscount squirmed beneath his uncle's piercing regard. The earl's attitude bordered on carping this evening. Or was it merely Dalsany's imagination? There was so much at stake here, he didn't wish anything to go wrong where his betrothal to Lucy was concerned. Being more used to criticism than commendation, however, it was likely he was worrying for naught.

"Did you fall in love at first sight?" This came

from the ever romantic Eglantine, and in a more logical vein, Edith addressed her brother: "I don't know about Lucy, but you certainly must have fallen in love with her the very first moment you met."

The earl shot a censorious glance first at Eglantine, then at Edith. "This conversation is verging on offensive," he admonished, although the truth was the twins were asking the precise questions he himself wished to hear answered.

"Oh, Uncle Alex," pouted the gypsy-haired twin. "Lucy doesn't mind, do you? She's going to be our sister after all. And we shan't have any secrets."

Lucy schooled her smile to remain in place. Although she wasn't usually shy of the truth—my goodness, look at how she'd opened up to Anthony when they'd met in the garden at Exeter House—the mention of secrets and falling in love made her exceedingly uncomfortable. The worst of it was that she didn't even know how to answer Eglantine's question. She must be in love with Dalsany, she told herself, or why else would she have accepted his proposal?

Lady Bronwen resumed the lead in the conversation. "Tell me, Lucy, you said you were sponsored by a friend's mother, but what of your own parents, my dear?"

"Lucy's mother died when she was an infant, and her father when she was barely eight," supplied the viscount, who was beginning to wish his sweet Lucy had a bit more experience in life. If his family didn't behave, they were liable to frighten her off.

"Oh, Lucy, we've so much in common," exclaimed Edith. "So did ours! Our parents, that is. Perish when we were small."

"But Edith and I had each other," said Eglantine. "Oh, dearest Lucy, who did you have?"

To her horror, Lucy almost turned to the earl, but she managed to control herself, and merely replied, "There was Mademoiselle and my governess, Miss Beall, and the other girls. In particular, there was Lady Margaret."

"The other girls?" queried Edith.

"Pray, Lucy, don't tell me you grew up at a boarding school."

"Eglantine!" said the earl in stern admonishment.

"Oh, it really wasn't that dreadful. Unlike the other students I had my own little cottage at the edge of a cherry orchard, and my pony was stabled at a nearby farm. It was rather like having two score of sisters."

"And you must have had oodles of invitations each holiday."

"Why, just imagine, you've probably seen every county in England."

"And the Highlands, too?"

"No, not the Highlands, and not even half of England. The only county I've visited is Norfolk." She saw the twins' disappointment and amended rather apologetically, "You see, I spent most of my holidays at the academy."

Out of the blue, an image of another dining room came to Lucy's mind. Upon her mental canvas she saw the treasured memory of Lady Margaret's brothers and sisters about the Christmas table at Mersham Castle. In the next moment, however, this vision was replaced by the reality of the sight before her. Slowly, her gaze moved about the table, resting in turn upon each member of the Paget family.

"Miss Wickham, is your veal cold?" The earl's query broke into her contemplation.

Lucy startled and momentarily focused upon the medallions in mushroom sauce before her, then she raised her eyes to the earl's face and detected the first sign of a thaw on his granite expression. "It's fine. Quite delicious, in fact," she replied, and a second more crimson blush heated her cheeks. "I was merely caught up in a thought."

"And what was that?" inquired the viscount. "Nothing too dreadful, I trust, for you were looking at the lot of us as if we'd grown six heads and turned to Medusa."

Horrified that she might have made such an unfavorable impression, the truth spilled forth. "I was merely thinking that this is only the second family with whom I've dined." She didn't intend to sound pitiful or lost, and she quickly studied their expressions. The viscount and his sisters appeared to be considering this confidence, while Lady Bronwen gave Lucy a kind smile and told her that it made her arrival all the more special. As for the earl, his expression had once again hardened; mayhap, Lucy decided with regret, there had never been a change in the first place.

"Only the second?" Eglantine was visibly moved by Lucy's revelation. "But didn't you have friends other than your schoolmates?"

"Egad, haven't you any sense?" snapped the viscount. Miss Lucy Wickham was supposed to be the young lady for whom all would envy him his good fortune, not some peculiarity of upbringing who would elicit morbid curiosity. For Lucy's sake, he told himself, he'd have to speak with the twins before they spread every detail of Lucy's background up and down the coast. She was going to have to live at Clovelly, and there was no sense in starting off with any untoward chitchat.

Lucy ignored the viscount's outburst as her mind focused on pleasant memories. "Well, yes, now that you ask, I did have one special friend. He used to visit a nearby estate." Her hand flew upward as if to snatch back these dreamily spoken words, but it was too late and everyone's curiosity had been aroused.

"He?" The viscount's brow rose.

"A beau?" inquired Eglantine on a sigh.

Lucy chose her next words with care. "Nothing so exciting. I was a schoolgirl and he was merely a kindly gentleman." Feeling the earl's gaze upon her, Lucy forced herself to look in his direction. He was frowning, but there was something else about his expression, a certain melancholy. Had he remembered? Her heart leapt at the prospect, and in as nonchalant a tone as was possible she added, "He came each August for several weeks, and I would climb over the orchard wall to visit with him on the beach."

"But how ever did you meet this gentleman in the first place?"

"He rescued me from drowning."

Eglantine clutched her hand to her bosom and heaved a dramatic sigh. "And he was tall and dark and handsome and you were leagues in love with him. Am I right?"

"Don't be silly," said the viscount, who didn't appreciate the thought of his Lucy in connection with some other gentleman. "Lucy was only a child."

Eglantine's suggestion, however, was frightfully close to the truth, and Lucy feared the sudden pallor upon her cheeks would betray her.

Thank goodness Edith asked a question of her own.

"Oh, Lucy, tell us, does this mean you know how to swim?"

"Of course," Lucy replied, heedless of the fact that proper young ladies did not swim, or at least, if they did, they would never admit to such a talent.

No one, however, appeared shocked by this intelligence. In point of fact, the twins were ecstatic.

"Then you can swim with us, for Grandmother won't let us go to the plunge pool alone, and Anthony doesn't swim and Uncle Alex won't take us anymore."

"I should like to do that," Lucy said, while her thoughts were focused upon the earl. What was he thinking, she wondered? Perhaps he was beginning to remember, and she glanced his way, but there was no indication that this was the case. He was staring at his nieces, and there was no particular expression upon his countenance. The conversation could have been about the merits of hens' eggs versus pullets' for the lack of reaction he displayed.

"Uncle Alex is the one who taught us. All the Paget women swim," declared Edith.

Lucy continued to study the earl, but even this remark failed to make an impression upon him.

"How did you learn to swim, Lucy?" asked Eglantine.

Surely now he would recall, thought Lucy, as she modulated her voice to remain calm. "It was the man who rescued me. He taught me to swim." She wanted to add, *But it was more than that. Much more. Oh, how I cherished his company. How I yearned for July to turn to August. How I scarcely ate or slept in anticipation of his return.* But she couldn't. The thought of how little their relationship had meant to him was pushing her perilously close to tears, and she paid undue attention to the last three mushrooms on her dinner plate.

Once more Eglantine sighed, and Lady Bronwen took up the conversation.

"It's a lovely story. Are you and this gentleman still acquainted?"

"No, ma'am." Once more she wondered what the expression upon the earl's face might be, but she dared not look his way. "One summer he stopped coming, and I never saw him again. I didn't even know his name."

"Ah, yes, and 'tis likely for the better," declared the viscount with a note of finality.

At this, the earl knew a stab of annoyance. Dalsany acted as if *he* knew what was best for Lucy, and quite frankly, the earl was beginning to believe that wasn't possible. He studied Lucy's face in profile. She had grown into a young woman of uncommon beauty. Her golden hair was as full and curly as it had been that last summer, but was worn now in a loose coil at the nape of her neck. Her complexion was fairer than he recalled, paler even than when she had entered the dining room, the high color having faded from her cheeks, and there were, he noted, signs of strain about her eyes and mouth.

It was evident that she was troubled about something, he concluded, which led him to a second and even more significant assumption: her memory of those August days was as vivid as his. He heard her sweet voice—*I believe I'd like to marry you, sir, if you please*—and the knot in his chest tightened. It didn't matter that her affection had been nothing more than a lonely schoolgirl's adoration, her disappointment must have been acute when he left without a farewell, and he knew a profound guilt that he had hurt her in any way.

He wanted to reach across the table to take her hand in his, to pull her from her chair and hold her to him, tell her he was sorry. *I won't hurt you again. I promise. No one will ever hurt you again, dear minx. Everything's going to be all right. I'll see to it.* Of course, he couldn't say or do any of that, and so he sat at the head of the twelve-foot table, his emotions locked inside, his pain and guilt burning without relief.

The plates were cleared away by a trio of footmen, the conversation switched to horses during the venison, and then the gentlemen discussed the politics of war during the artichoke bottoms.

The meal was almost over, cabinet pudding and crème Italienne had been served, when the dowager countess said, "I hope you don't mind so soon after arriving at Clovelly, but several of our neighbors shall be joining us for tea tomorrow afternoon."

"That sounds lovely," said Lucy. "I should like to meet your friends."

"I must apologize ahead of time. But when word got out that our Anthony had become affianced there was more than one curiosity seeker upon our doorstep, and my small get-together has rather multiplied."

"Indeed, Lucy, news of your betrothal has been quite the *on dit*. No one ever thought Anthony would marry," Edith divulged.

"He's such a rake, y'know," said Eglantine.

Both the earl and the viscount were glowering at these remarks. Neither of the twins noticed, and Eglantine babbled on.

"And Lady Priscilla Fox Strangways was positively undone when she heard the news. You do remember her, don't you, Anthony?"

"Can't say as I do," he replied, although he knew the surname well, and surmised the chit's father had to be the Earl of Ilchester, whose family owned much of the nearby village of Abbotsbury. More than likely she was one of his sisters' spotty friends who used to hover about the nursery and emit high-pitched giggles whenever he was in sight.

"She drove her rig over and cried buckets when the announcement was published in the *Times*," supplied Edith.

Eglantine expanded, "Went into a veritable grizzle."

A flush of vanity fanned across the viscount's cheeks. It was rather pleasing to consider that some young lady, albeit spotty and nothing more exciting than an acquaintance of his sisters', having harbored a secret *tendre* for him, was reduced to tears at the news he was to marry.

"Lady Priscilla said she'd gladly trade her sapphire earbobs to switch places with Lucy."

"She said whoever Lucy Wickham was she was the luckiest girl in the world."

"Lady Priscilla is correct. I am very lucky," Lucy told her soon-to-be family, fancying that next year at this time there might be a new baby in the nursery.

The viscount beamed like a popinjay, causing the earl to feel extremely out of sorts. Finding he could remain silent no longer, the earl set his wine goblet on the table and coughed twice in a way designed to command attention.

"Miss Wickham lucky? Have you all gone mad?" He stared daggers at the viscount and spoke without any effort to mask his cynicism. "I doubt my undeserving nephew knows how truly blessed he is." He rose abruptly, the majordomo rushed forward to hand his cane to him, and before the astonished onlookers, he quit the dining room without another word and proceeded to his private study, where he closeted himself for the remainder of the night with two bottles of smuggled brandy.

Pungent white smoke filled the thatched cottage, and Edith covered her nose when she entered beneath the low door. The first order of business was to open the shutters and ventilate the cottage. No matter what Nanny Swinburne had claimed, Edith didn't believe that smoked vervain root was going to aid in Captain Henry Pomeroy's recovery, and in an effort to swish some of the smoke outside, she vigorously moved her hands back and forth like ravens' wings. Having rendered the air somewhat less toxic, she went to a cot and stared at the pinched face of a man, his eyes closed, his complexion waxen, and his breathing so shallow it was barely discernible. She watched and waited until the slightest movement of his eyelids told her he was still alive.

Satisfied that her patient had survived another night, Edith moved away from the cot to place a basket on a crude table. For this visit she'd managed to collect shortbread triangles, fresh cheese, three boiled eggs, a handful of early strawberries, and a roasted chicken wing. As if it were a feast fit for a king, she displayed this offering upon a dented pewter platter. This required two attempts, for she wished it to appear plentiful and appetizing, and once done, she sat upon the bare floor to wait for Captain Pomeroy to open his eyes.

"Captain Pomeroy, are you feeling any better? I've brought you something to eat," Edith said in an encouraging way. Since being brought to this cottage a week before, the captain had neither opened his eyes nor uttered a syllable, but once Edith had heard Nanny Swinburne say it was beneficial for the ill to hear voices, and so Edith talked to the captain each time she visited. It helped with the healing process, the old nurse had professed, and this time, as if to prove this point, the captain's eyes opened and he stared at Edith.

"Who are you?" he asked in a weak raspy voice.

"Lady Edith Paget." She knelt down, slipped a hand beneath his head and held a glass of water to his lips.

"You're nothing more than a child," he said, the rasping gone and a bit more strength in his words.

"I've been keeping you alive," was her simple reply.

He nodded in respect. "The earl. Alex. He's—"

"He's my uncle, and right now he's gone to see Lord Forrester in Weymouth. Everyone thinks he's meeting with the estate manager, but it's his way of not letting on that he's working for the Foreign office. No one's the least bit suspicious about Uncle Alex or you."

"You appear to know a good deal about this."

"Uncle Alex trusts me."

"And so I suppose I must as well. How long have I been here?"

"Six days. I found you on the beach below the

cliffs, and you must know that I didn't have the foggiest idea what to think at first with all the talk of spies. You know, stumbling across a bleeding man isn't an everyday sort of occurrence, and I'd never seen a bullet wound before, but I surmised what it was and so I hid you beneath some gorse and went to fetch Uncle Alex. 'Course he knew right away who you were, said he'd been expecting you, and once we'd gotten you here and he'd taken the bullet from your shoulder he told me how important it was to make sure you lived.''

''You appear to have done a commendable job, Lady Edith. I must thank you for my life,'' he said, wondering how much of the truth the earl had told his niece.

''No, you shouldn't thank me. It was my duty.''

What an odd child, he thought, but then Harrow had always been a different sort of fellow. They'd been classmates down at Oxford, not particularly close, although they'd played cricket a few times at Bournemouth, and then their paths had crossed on the Peninsula. Both had been wounded, though Captain Pomeroy's injury had been nothing more than a saber nick to his thigh, and they were both now working for the Foreign Office. The earl was an intermediary between English agents on the Continent and the Foreign Office, and Captain Pomeroy was the only Englishman who could identify a double agent reputed to be in the district. Feeling a bit stronger, the captain glanced about the room and noticed the pewter salver. ''Is that food?''

''Shall I feed you?'' was Edith's eager reply.

''Do you mind?''

''Not at all.''

A weak smile turned up the corners of his

mouth. "It's your duty, of course." And when she sat beside him and held a bit of boiled egg to his lips, he asked, "Tell me about yourself, Lady Edith." She reminded him of his sister and home, and it pleased him to hear her talk as she broke off bits of chicken and shortbread and held up his head so he might drink more water. He hadn't eaten in a long time and the effort was exhausting, and the last thing he heard before drifting to sleep was part of a story about a motherless girl named Lucy who was as beautiful as an angel, and how this Lucy had tamed a rogue with the spirit of a devil.

Seven

"**Y**OU WISHED TO SEE ME, sir?" Dalsany hesitated on the threshold of the earl's study.

His uncle was standing before the hearth, leaning with one arm upon the carved mantel and staring at the cold embers. He hadn't changed from the clothes he'd worn the night before, his shirt was rumpled, and his neckcloth was nowhere to be seen. The scent of stale brandy clung to the air, and although it was well past noon, the room remained dark, the heavy brocade curtains being tightly drawn.

The earl cocked his head to one side to address the viscount. "Mr. Frith tells me you're a devotee of raw egg and bitters."

"On occasion," the viscount responded to this cryptic remark, wishing he could better read his uncle's mood. Interviews with the earl usually entailed a disagreement, which Dalsany usually lost, and now that he was so close to having things come together in his favor, he didn't appreciate the prospect of his uncle raking him over the coals for some meaningless indiscretion. Whatever he could have done to necessitate this particular interview was a mystery to Dalsany. He tried for a light tenor. "Despite the sound of it, its curative properties are remarkable."

The older gentleman grunted in reply, the meaning of which was lost upon Dalsany, and the tick tock of the mantel clock filled the silence between them. At length, the earl said, "Take a seat."

Dalsany complied, finding the nearest chair, from which he watched his uncle cross the study without the benefit of his cane.

Reaching a breakfront, the earl lounged in a casual manner against the heavy piece of furniture as he spoke. "I wished to discuss your forthcoming wedding."

This topic seemed safe, and Dalsany relaxed, stretching his legs out before him as he leaned back in the chair. "I intend to—that is, Lucy and I had hoped to be able to set a date as soon as possible."

"So I've discovered," the earl drawled, and produced from a drawer in the breakfront a sheaf of paper bearing an official seal in scarlet wax.

"It must be from Sir Lumley," the viscount said with confidence, referring to a distant relative who was a representative of the archbishop and therefore capable of issuing a special marriage license to dispense with the required calling of the banns. "What does he say? I wrote him, y'know, before Lucy and I left Town."

"He, of course, sends his felicitations, and asks that you not name a son in his honor. Lumley's been a formidable cross to bear, he writes."

"But what does he say of my request?" Dalsany queried, not bothering to staunch his impatience, which was a mistake.

The earl's countenance darkened. "It would be

simplest, I suppose, to lie and tell you that he refused.''

''I don't understand. Simplest?'' Dalsany knew a frisson of apprehension. ''What's your point?''

''My point, Anthony, is that whatever Sir Lumley decided is irrelevant. You'll wait the traditional time period, and the banns will be published for three consecutive Sundays at Saint Catherine's Chapel.'' Whereupon the earl held up the official-looking document and began to tear it first lengthwise, then crosswise.

Dalsany sprang to his feet and seized one of the shreds of paper off the floor. ''Egad, Uncle Alex! It's a special license. Have you gone mad? You must stop that.'' He grabbed a second and a third scrap. ''How dare you?''

''I dare because I'm still the head of this family, and I'll not countenance anything that might cause gossip. In case it had escaped your attention, let me point out that a special license would do just that. Cause gossip.'' He impaled the viscount with a rapier-thin gaze. ''There isn't any reason why you need to marry in haste, is there?''

''Nothing more than trying to comply with the codicil deadline.''

''That's why you're marrying her, isn't it?'' His hands curled into fists and he made himself ask, ''Because of the codicil?''

''What did you expect?'' Dalsany was on his knees, gathering up the torn special license, and he glanced up to quip, ''True love?''

In that instant, the earl was beset by a powerful urge to yank the viscount by the jacket lapels and shake him senseless, but he managed to control himself. ''Does she know about any of this?''

''You may be crazed, Uncle Alex, but I'm not.''

''You don't think you should tell her?'' the earl

asked, thinking as he watched Dalsany piecing together the special license as if it were a child's puzzle that they were both prime candidates for Bedlam.

The viscount frowned and wondered aloud, "What's this sudden interest in Lucy? She isn't even a member of the family. At least not yet."

"Precisely. She's an innocent young woman without any family to guide her, nor father to look after her interests, and it would be—"

"And you think I'm taking advantage of her." Clutching the remnants of the document, the viscount rose and declared in self-defense, "Well, she ain't no heiress, if that's what you're thinking. There was barely enough money left in her inheritance to see her through a Season. Lucy may have lived like royalty at that academy, but she needs to marry as much as I do."

"There are different ways of taking advantage, you know," the earl said in a voice so deadly serious it sounded like an unspoken threat.

"She's getting a bargain," Dalsany retorted in a rather petulant huff. "Besides which, I don't know why your nose is out of joint, Uncle Alex."

"It's very simple. You're not good enough for her."

Dalsany bristled like a hedgehog. "I may be a smidge rickety when it comes to faro or hazard, and I've never been good at keeping up with my accounts, but I'm not queer in the attic, nor captive to some perverse pleasure of the night. Egad, Uncle Alex, not good enough, you say. Why every summer a flock of girls marry far worse than myself and make a go of it. Females know how to manage such things, you know." This argument did not appear to produce any positive effect upon the earl, and Dalsany, owing to increasing trepidation, gave voice to the unthinkable question: "You're not going to tell her about the codicil, are you?"

"No, I don't think so," the earl responded after a few moments' consideration. "If the young woman was foolish enough to fall in love with you, I shan't be the one to break her heart."

Dalsany breathed a sigh of relief, and knowing it was prudent to show an agreeable face, he said, "Of course, Uncle Alex, we'll do it by the letter. A few extra weeks of waiting to wed can't do any harm. In fact, it's probably best to postpone Grandmother's gala until the reading of the banns. That should scotch any gossip." He pocketed the shredded license, gave an abbreviated bow, and departed before his uncle might change his mind.

After several moments, the earl moved away from the breakfront and walked to the window. Using his cane, he separated the curtains, and the first rays of midday sun spilled into the study, causing him to squint most dreadfully. It required a full minute for his good eye to adjust to the bright light, after which he gazed into the garden, catching sight of Lucy and the twins on the adjacent brickwork terrace.

A rectangular pool dominated the terrace, and amidst statuary of leaping dolphins a miniature yacht—the name *Miss Lucy* emblazoned in gold lettering upon the stern—glided across the water.

Lucy and Edith were hatless, their dress sleeves had been pushed up to the elbows, and more than likely they were barefoot as well, the earl thought, remembering how the child Lucy had loved the sensation of cool water upon her bare toes. This afternoon, Lucy's hair was not pinned up, rather it had been combed out to be held in place by a forest green ribbon that matched the color of her dress; the earl knew it was the exact same green shade as her eyes and he wished that he was closer, for he was sure those lovely eyes were sparkling with merriment and he couldn't prevent himself from wishing that he might share a small measure of that pleasure. An odd little tug of jealousy pulled at him.

Their voices drifted upward, and although he strained to hear, he couldn't make out what it was they were saying. Their actions, however, spoke volumes. Eglantine secured her bonnet beneath her chin and gave her head a ladylike shake, whereupon Lucy lifted the hem of her skirt to reveal a bare foot, which she dipped in the water. The sailboat floated by and she pushed it back out toward the middle of the pool. Edith followed suit, standing on the adjacent ledge, and there they stood, pushing the sailboat back and forth between them with their feet. Despite their laughter and obvious enjoyment, Eglantine didn't participate in this less than decorous pursuit; at length, Lucy motioned to Eglantine to join them, but the dark-haired twin remained at a respectable distance.

Unnoticed by the earl, the study door opened and closed. He was remembering another time and place and how he'd taught a yellow-haired girl to handle the tiller in a small fishing boat. *I think I should like to sail around the world and see where the tea leaves grow and worms spin silk and maharajas ride on elephants' backs. I'm sure it's a wondrous sight. Would you take me, Pip? And we could live off flying fish and mussels and never have to wake up before sunrise again.* She was a delightful companion, and he'd been tempted to make her fancy a reality. Wrapped up in this pleasant memory, he didn't hear Lady Bronwen's muted footfall, nor was he aware of her presence in the study until she placed a hand upon his forearm in greeting.

He acknowledged his mother with a nod, but neither of them spoke. In companionable silence, they watched the girls, and when Lucy had succeeded in coaxing Eglantine to take off her shoes and stockings to test the water, Lady Bronwen reflected, "Miss Lucy Wickham is someone very special. Quite a remarkable young lady, I believe."

"Yes, she is," the earl agreed, an uncharacteristically wistful quality lacing his voice. His gaze didn't waver from the activity at the fountain, in particular from the slender young woman in forest green. What if he'd never been wounded and had continued to make the rounds each Season? What if he'd never named Dalsany heir? He couldn't deny the question: Would his future be different? He couldn't stop himself wondering: Would he have been the one to bring Lucy Wickham home to Clovelly?

Lady Bronwen studied her son's expression. "She's special to you. Isn't she?"

"You never cease to amaze me, Mother." There wasn't an ounce of emotion in this statement. "I could almost believe in witchcraft."

"What's so amazing?" she asked, her Highland brogue sounding stronger than it had moments before. " 'Tis no witchcraft or trickery, for where there is love it requires no extraordinary powers of observation to see the truth."

He was taken aback by her mention of love, and "You're mistaken" was his all-too-hasty rejoinder.

"I don't think so. Enow." She offered a gentle

smile, the heavy burr eased from her voice. "Although how it would have happened or why I'm not sure. I do have theory. Would like to hear it?"

In spite of himself, an expression that almost resembled a grin teased the edges of the earl's mouth. "Do I really have any choice?"

"You were that gentleman on the beach."

The earl's silence confirmed his mother's supposition, and leaning more heavily than usual upon the cane, he was compelled to say, "Yes, Mother, I was that man on the beach, but I wasn't in love with her then any more than I might be now."

The lines upon Lady Bronwen's countenance reflected her skepticism.

"It is merely as you said, Mother; she is special, and one does not easily forget someone like that," he essayed to dismiss the subject, but failing to produce even the vaguest impact upon the dowager countess's doubtful expression, he was compelled to offer another explanation.

"You know, I was young myself when I pulled her out of the surf, just barely out of Oxford. Perhaps older in years, but you remember me then, shallow and concerned with little else except living life to its fullest. The set I moved with was jaded and fast and thoroughly devoid of conscience or innocence, and she was the exact opposite. She was an amusing escape from Lady Anne and the others at Battersea Hall." After a momentary pause, he added, "To her, everything was new and wonderful. Everything—even I—had some virtue. I could scarcely believe someone saw the good in me, and her companionship was like an addictive elixir, for she never wanted anything more of me than what I gave. She gave of herself without any obligation. Or at least that's what I thought.

"But the third summer it changed." He ran a hand through his hair, his regard never wavering from Lucy on the brickwork terrace below. "That third August I began to see how she depended upon me. There was no one else in her life except for hired governesses and the school staff, a fact which quite frightened me. That August I left earlier than usual, and soon after I broke off my liaison with Lady Anne. I never returned to Battersea Hall."

He paused, but Lady Bronwen, knowing this was not the full story, waited for him to finish. Outside, the girls laughed, the mood was happy, but the lines upon her son's face deepened. At length, he went on.

"Time passed, and there was the campaign on the Peninsula and my injury, and during all of that, it was always her image that took away the loneliness. She became important to me, and for some insane reason which I'll never understand I made a pledge to find her after it was over. Verily, there were days when I believe I survived just to uphold that pledge.

"But everything was changed when I finally returned." He paused, and of its own volition, a hand rose to touch the black patch covering his eye. After a few moments, his hand fell away. Slowly, he shook his head as if to deny his foolishness. "I realized she wouldn't be a child anymore, running barefoot on the beach and looking for a summer playmate. She'd be a young woman, graduated from the academy and gone out into the world, looking for a husband and a life of her own, and she'd be much too sheltered and innocent for a fallen soldier disillusioned by pain, fear, and defeat.''

Weariness crept into his voice. ''I don't know why I ever made such a promise to myself. Maybe I thought I could turn back the clock and relive those summer days. Maybe I thought I could be young and whole once more, and I could start over again, if only I could find her. You see, I'd made her the key to my survival and my future. It was foolish, I know, for we can't turn back time. We can never change what's been done.''

''Yet here she is,'' Lady Bronwen concluded. She knew a profound concern for her son and she blinked away the tears pooling in her eyes. Having suffered much already, there was scant joy in his life, and it was disturbing to listen to his confession and realize that he didn't understand the meaning of his feelings toward Lucy. Sorrow touched her eyes and voice, when she gently asked, ''What do you propose to do, Alex? Have you thought about that?''

''Welcome her to her new home and family, and make sure she is happy.'' He didn't hesitate in this reply. ''Marriage to Dalsany won't be pleasant. He'll abandon her here at Clovelly, y'know, and jaunt off to London as soon as they're wed. He'll never be able to resist the lure of the hells and his light o' loves. If I could stop the wedding, I would, but I won't, not as long as she loves him.''

''But you'll be here to step in when Anthony is gone and be a friend to his wife.''

''I hadn't thought it through, but yes, that's right. He'll be off to London, but I shall be here to see Lucy through. She won't be lonely or lack for companionship as long as I can help it.''

The melancholy upon Lady Bronwen's face

grew more pronounced. "My dear Alex, you know life isn't that simple. It won't work out that way, and it grieves me to think how hurt you and Lucy shall both be before this is over."

The earl tried to make light of what his mother had said. "I can't believe that's you talking. Far too much romantic twaddle for the respected Dowager Countess of Harrow. If you're not more careful, Mother, we shall soon begin mistaking you for Eglantine."

Lady Bronwen frowned. The timepiece on the mantel chimed four and a sailing ship set in the clock face rocked back and forth on a green enamel sea. "Will you be joining us for tea, Alex?"

"I don't think so."

"Another meeting with the estate manager?"

"Something like that."

Reaching out to her grown son, the dowager countess let the back of her hand rest against his cheek in a gesture that revealed the intensity of her maternal concern. "Always be honest with yourself, Alex. You must never forget that."

"Of course," he promised his mother, while silently he made himself another promise. If ever Lucy gave him the slightest hint that she remembered, he would reveal himself. Yes, he would be honest, if given the chance, and yes, he was a patient man and was willing to wait for as long as necessary.

With a satisfied smile Lady Bronwen kissed her son upon the cheek and left the study to receive her guests in the gold salon.

The earl returned his attention to Lucy and the twins. Their sandals were back on, their dress sleeves rolled down and neatly fastened at the wrists, and they were mounting the terrace steps to the gold salon. Lucy looked up and spotted him. Their gazes met and he gave a terse nod.

"Good afternoon, sir," she called out, her voice carefree and clear and gay, no trace of the monumental effort it required to address him as if they were new acquaintances.

And before he might stop himself, he called back, "Yes, it is a good afternoon," a long-forgotten spontaneity in this response. It was as if a miracle had reordered time and they were back in Sussex, and for one heart-stopping moment the earl feared that what his mother had said about love was true. In the next instant, however, he realized that the peculiar queasiness in his midsection could be attributed to nothing more threatening than last night's impulsive overindulgence in brandy.

Twelve of the neighborhood's most distinguished ladies and their assorted female offspring sipped Lapsang souchong and nibbled jellied sandwiches while the viscount, positioned beside Lucy as if she were a prized hunting trophy, regaled this rapt audience with a litany of her merits. Lucy was beginning to feel like the tamed monkey in a sultan's harem when Lady Priscilla Fox Strangways was announced. Whatever Dalsany had been about to say regarding Lucy's abilities as a horsewoman was caught in his throat as Lady Priscilla, overdressed for a country tea in a dampened muslin gown with a revealing bodice and ruched sleeves that had been pulled off the shoulders, sashayed into the gold salon.

More than one pair of eyebrows arched in censure at this brazen display, while the viscount, looking for all the world like a hound ready to pounce upon a juicy bone, offered Lady Priscilla the seat nearest the settee. Someone attempted to make polite conversation about how calm the seas had been this spring.

"Not at all good for the maintenance of public safety, y'know," remarked Lady Asquith, and everyone knew precisely what she meant.

Although the beaches of Lyme Bay were rugged, local residents remained unconvinced of this natural protection, and one and all, they were enthralled by the fear of a French invasion. Despite his early winter defeat on the Russian front, Bonaparte had not only raised a new army but was once more threatening the sanctity of the British coastline. Lookouts were posted on every hilltop from Kent to Cornwall, and locally, tourists to the pleasure town of Weymouth were subject to unusual if not outright hostile scrutiny. After all, anyone could be one of Boney's agents.

"You don't suppose *it* could happen again?" Lady Caroline Legg spoke in such a tone that a stranger would conclude she possessed personal experience with foreign invasion, for as was local habit Lady Caroline carried on as if the Danish conquest of the coastline had occurred within her recent memory, rather than nearly a thousand years before.

"It would not hurt to be on our guard. If nothing else, *he* is resilient," remarked Lady Bronwen.

Even the vaguest reference to Bonaparte caused reticules to open and recuperative salts to be employed by the faint of heart.

"Quite, quite. We must be prepared. Fresh timbers were found below the cliffs the other morning." This from Lady Flyte, who had a fondness for being the bearer of news. If one wished to know any of the goings-on in the neighborhood one need ask no further than Lady Flyte. Nothing escaped her ear or eye, and on more than one occasion the lady had actually been caught eavesdropping. "One of our tenants found the wreckage and reported the whole if it to Sir Arthur Kemp, who visited Lord Forrester in Weymouth."

"Lord Forrester is in Weymouth, whatever for?"

Lady Flyte supplied, "*On dit* there's an assassin within our midst. A double agent."

More recuperative salts were dispensed, and a frantic debate ensued, several ladies insisting the wreckage was nothing more than the latest evidence of local smugglers while others asserted it was proof positive there was a French spy in their midst. Only one guest, the Duchess of Mitford, did not participate in the exchange. Instead, her grace, who had remained silent until this moment, addressed Lucy in an aside:

"Got your mother's height, do you, gel?"

Lucy was taken aback by the implication of this question. Her throat grew suddenly dry, and for several heartbeats she stared, gape-mouthed, at the reed-thin ancient before she might inquire, "Did you know my mother, your grace?"

"What was that?" She raised a gnarled hand to her ear and leaned closer to Lucy. The Duchess of Mitford, who bore a striking resemblance to a small gray bird, was nearing the end of her eighth decade. She could barely hear or see and had been crippled since the age of sixty-two when Charlie's Bonnie Lassie had refused a fence and the duchess had landed in a ditch, yet it was a point of immense personal pride that she continued to make daily visits about the countryside, despite the fact that she made these visits upon a lacquered sedan chair in Chinese red and usually fell asleep before her host or hostess had served refreshments. Today was a notable exception, for her grace had been propped upon her nest of pillows, staring most pointedly at Lucy for the past forty minutes.

"Did you know my mother?" repeated Lucy in hopeful expectation. "I never knew her myself, you see. Although my father believed we favored one another."

"And where's he now?" her grace demanded as if she were acquainted with the people about whom she was talking.

"Both of my parents are deceased."

"Ah, yes, well, we all look forward to that fate, don't we?"

Acutely aware of the cool touch of her mother's locket beneath the bodice of her gown, Lucy asked, "Did you know them, ma'am? My parents?"

"What was your name, gel?" the duchess chirped, then answered the question herself. "Lucy Wickham, wasn't it? No, can't say I ever knew them. Ain't no Wickhams hereabouts."

It seemed her grace had succumbed to a lapse of concentration, as was common with the elderly. Lucy looked to the viscount for his opinion only to discover that the gentleman was so engrossed in conversation with Lady Priscilla that he could not have heard a word exchanged between herself and the gray lady upon the lacquered sedan chair.

"It would mean a great deal to me to learn of my parents," Lucy confided to the duchess.

"I thought you said they were dead," was the ancient's rejoinder as her eyelids closed and she appeared to drift into sleep.

Lucy bit back the urge to utter some hideously

unladylike exclamation. Frustrated and disappointed by this pointless exchange, she turned back to Dalsany and was about to inject herself into the conversation between her fiancé and Lady Priscilla when the Duchess of Mitford opened her eyes and spoke once more.

"Perhaps you would join me for tea. Tuesday next at Aylesbury."

"Thank you, ma'am. I should like that."

Whereupon a slew of other invitations were issued. There was to be a formal dinner with Lord and Lady Asquith at their town house on the waterfront before the next Weymouth assembly, and not to be outdone, there would be a musicale of military marches at Moonfleet Manor in honor of Lady Flyte's grandson's promotion to the rank of colonel in the Horse Guards, and, of course, there were the usual array of country dinners, picnics, and an outing on one of the nearby sea lochs. It appeared Lucy had been accepted without incident into the fold of local society.

Eight

❦ ❦ ❦ ❦

DUSK ON THE DORSET CLIFFS was never twice the same. There were evenings when a misty quiet sunset fell over the landscape, the terns swooped down on gentle winds, and little waves rolled pebbled against the shore, and there were nights such as this when the line of white foam extended westward from Portland to Devon and the sea swallows hid from angry jackdaws buffeted from their cliffside nests by a mounting wind. As with any nightfall the colors were spectacular.

Lucy had never seen anything quite like it before. There were gold and orange cliffs layering down to gray, and blue cliffs dotted with yellow horned poppies and crimson yarrows. There was the dark green stretch of Burton Mere, where the reeds sheltered marsh birds, and there was a curving coastline that was turning to purple before Lucy's eyes.

The wind teased her, pushing Lucy forward, then pulling her back, and the skirt of her gown snapped about her legs as she followed a worn path along the cliff. She walked for several minutes and when she stopped to glance over her shoulder she was surprised at how far she'd come, for only the chimney pots of Clovelly were visible. But that was not her only surprise. About twenty yards along the path a figure was heading toward her. It was a man, and from the slightly uneven walk she knew it was the earl.

She waited as he neared, wondering what he was doing here. Following dinner, the family had adjourned to the paneled library, where Edith had challenged Dalsany to a game of draughts while Eglantine scanned a pile of newspapers for clippings to paste in her scrapbook, and the earl and Lady Bronwen took up their reading, *The Times* for the earl, and a copy of Miss Austen's latest novel for the dowager countess. Lucy had tried to entertain herself with *La Belle Assemble*, but finding it impossible to concentrate she had excused herself. Military themes were the latest fashion rage, but satin and fringe epaulets were of little interest to Lucy when there was the unanswered question of whether or not the Duchess of Mitford could tell her anything about her mother. And, of course, there was the earl. He'd been watching her, she was certain of it, over the top of the newspaper, and his scrutiny had been more than she could abide, hence she'd quit the library under the pretense of fetching her shawl.

Passing through the vast marble rotunda at the rear of the great house and hearing the echo of the waves, she'd been drawn outside and across the lawns to the cliff walk. A stroll seemed a perfect alternative to returning to the library, and her preoccupation with matters worrisome had faded away during the solitary walk. Ironically, her escape was about to be intruded upon by one of the reasons she had sought retreat in the first place.

The earl reached her side. He wore the constant somber expression she had come to expect of the

Earl of Harrow, but his voice was warm and gentle. To her astonishment, he sounded like his younger self, like the Pip she had once trusted and adored. "I thought I might find you here."

Her heart skipped a beat, and she said the first thing that came to mind. "It's breathtaking out here. I feel as if I've come home."

"To the sea?"

"Yes, to the sea," she replied, struck by the impression that there was something more to his innocent query. Her heart continued its erratic pace, and seized by the delightful fantasy that this wasn't the earl, but Pip, she wondered what harm might come of it if she allowed herself to pretend this was Pip, to relax and talk freely with him. On the other hand, it could be dangerous. This gentleman affected her the way no other man, not even the viscount, did, and although Lucy wasn't sure what it meant, she didn't need anyone to tell her that it wasn't in the least bit proper.

"Would you like to walk a bit farther, Miss Wickham? Soon it will be dark. The cliff isn't safe then." He offered his arm.

Lucy hesitated. "Do you think it's appropriate?"

"Why ever not?"

"We're unchaperoned and—"

"And you are betrothed to my nephew," he said in such a way that it sounded perfectly all right. Again, the earl offered Lucy his arm, and this time, she accepted. They continued in a westward direction. Glancing sideways at her profile, he wondered if the impetuous child had grown into a restrained young woman. "Tell me, Miss Wickham, do you always worry this much?"

"No."

"Ah, then, it must be me. Do I make you nervous?"

"Oh, no!" The fervor of this reply rather belied its veracity, and Lucy could not prevent the pink blush that tinted her cheeks.

Silence fell between them. After a dip in the path, he led her downhill to the edge of the cliff, where he pointed down the coastline with his cane. "That's Golden Cap and Lyme Harbor, where the Duke of Monmouth landed to wrest the throne from James. And beyond, there's Star Point in Devon."

"Devon? But that's miles away."

"Almost seventy, I believe."

"And such a clear view for such a distance. I can't imagine how a single French vessel could be so bold to sail into the bay and its passengers come ashore undetected."

"Can I assume from that remark that the ladies talked of Boney at tea?"

"Yes, and spies."

One ink-black brow rose in query.

Lucy clarified. "Apparently, some wreckage was discovered on the beach, and the ladies are fearful there's an assassin in our midst."

"And their mood? Was it verging on hysteria?"

"Not quite. Though I trust there's a plentiful supply of smelling salts at the local apothecary to tide them through the summer months."

Without warning a distant crack of thunder rent the night air followed by an ominous rumbling, and to Lucy's horror an expression of extreme alarm transformed the earl's face.

"Watch out, Minx. A cliff fall!"

With lightning speed, he gripped her arm, pulled her to him, and in the next second, he flung the two of them several feet away from the spot where they'd been standing at the edge of the cliff. They staggered for two or three paces before falling to the ground just as a portion of the cliff split away and tumbled to the sea below. It was a cliff fall, a natural occurrence up and down the Dorset coast, and although they occurred more frequently in the rainy winter months, they could happen anytime.

Trembling like a leaf, Lucy required several moments to calm herself. At first, all she could think was that she had almost died and Pip had saved her life. The enormity of that narrow escape was as overwhelming as her physical reaction to those moments of terror, but as her mind began to clear and her heart stilled, Lucy became aware of two more things. The first was that the earl had called her Minx, and second, they were still sprawled upon the ground in a most indecent jumble of legs and starched white petticoats, a situation that did not contribute to catching her breath.

"What did you say?" There was a measure of wonder in this query as she tilted her head to the side. He was lying on his back staring at the sky, and he didn't answer. "What did you call me?" she asked again, breathless and hardly daring to believe what she'd heard.

The earl remained silent. He had not intended this to happen. He had intended to wait for some hint from her before bringing back the past, and for one heart-stopping moment, he feared it was a terrible mistake, that somehow Lucy wasn't the girl from the beach, but when he dared to look at her the emotions upon her face banished his every doubt. There was no pity or repugnance, nor loathing or distrust, rather her great green eyes were shining with hope and the unmistakable light of affection. His chest contracted with bittersweet agony, and he replied in a low voice, "Minx. I called you Minx."

Tears slipped form Lucy's eyes to trail down her cheeks mixing with smudges of dirt and leaving thin dark streaks. She rose on one elbow to better see the whole of his strong handsome face. "Oh, Pip, my dearest Pip. Why didn't you say anything earlier?"

"Why didn't you?" he managed to parry, trying to inject a lighter tone as he untangled his legs from hers and supported himself in a half-sitting position.

"That's not fair to answer my question with another."

"No, it's not." He paused and again glanced to the gloaming sky. "I was caught unawares. It's that simple. I wasn't prepared to see you again, and certainly not on the front steps of Clovelly with an audience of family along with every servant who'd ever been in the employ of my mother. Besides, as a gentleman I don't wish to cause a rift between you and Anthony. After all, Edith did paint a rather romantic gilt upon the whole affair."

"And my fiancé has a jealous streak?"

"You didn't know?"

"No," she said, thinking that she didn't really know Dalsany all that well and the better she did the less she liked him. But she didn't utter a word of this. It would make her look fickle and shallow, and she wanted Pip's approbation. That was, she had suddenly discovered, important to her.

"But come, let's not worry about Anthony for now." He moved to a full upright position and helped her to sit beside him. He forced himself to say, "He shall have you for a lifetime, but right now this little reunion should be ours alone."

A funny little melting feeling wrapped its way around Lucy, and she whispered, "Yes." He couldn't have said anything that would have pleased her more, and all the misunderstandings and hurt were forgiven in that moment. Here was her old friend Pip, not the Earl of Harrow, nor the cruel stranger who'd left Sussex without a word. Still she couldn't help feeling shy. Perhaps it was the passage of time. A pretty shell pink blush colored her cheeks, and she angled her head sideways to peek at him from beneath thick lashes.

"Look at you," he marveled as he allowed himself the pleasure of framing her face with his hands while taking in the sight of her angelic face.

"I've grown up, haven't I?" She tried for a light tone, anything to mask her awareness of his scrutiny, anything to take her mind off the warmth of his gentle touch.

"Indeed, you've grown up quite nicely." He watched in fascination as Lucy's blush deepened and a grin turned up at the corners of her mouth. This sweet smile was achingly familiar, and the earl recalled the way she'd posed and turned for him in a tidal pool. Even now after all these years he remembered the jonquil-yellow dress and how her bonnet had dangled down her back and the wind had tousled her curls. At last, the memory and reality were one, and with that, the lines about his eyes and upon his forehead seemed to vanish, the tense set of his jaw was no more, and he smiled at Lucy.

Not once since she'd arrived at Clovelly had Lucy seen anything that resembled a smile touch the earl's somber expression, and now it was a miracle to see his mood so altered and to witness a genuine smile that softened his mouth and warmed his deep blue gaze. Lucy emitted a tiny cry of delight, then without consideration for propriety or the consequences she did the only thing that seemed right. She threw herself into Pip's arms and hugged him as tightly as she could, whereupon an even greater miracle happened— his smile turned to laughter, deep and free as the waves crashing on the beach below.

"Ah, but you haven't changed that much after all. Impulsive as always, I fear," he bantered, but teasing did not erase the effect Lucy was having upon him. Her proximity, the delicate fragrance of lemon-washed hair, the soft touch of blond curls against his cheek, and the even more tantalizing feel of round breasts pressing against his chest were unbearable. He was reacting to Lucy in a most masculine and entirely improper manner. Egads, she was affianced to his nephew. Furthermore, she trusted him, and such feelings were entirely out of place. Gently, he set her at arm's length.

"Suppose you simply tell me why you were out here alone. Didn't anyone tell you how dangerous the path can be? Cliff falls are an all too frequent occurrence."

"No, they didn't," she replied, swallowing in a dry throat. Her heart was beating a furious tattoo, her palms were suddenly and unaccountably moist. The last time she'd felt Pip's arms around her this hadn't happened, but she was no longer a child, rather she was a young woman who was acutely aware of him as a man, and although he held her away from him the pungent scent of cloves lingered in her nostrils and her body tingled where only seconds before they had touched. Apprehension seized her. She knew Pip would never hurt her, yet she was afraid, and moving away from him, she essayed a nonchalant smile. "But then I don't suppose anyone thought I'd go jaunting about by myself."

To which he thought, *And that's all the proof I need to be sure Anthony doesn't know Lucy as a man ought to know his future wife.* While his thoughts were of the mismatched couple, he merely said, "But why did you come?"

"To think."

"Ah, yes, of course, I should have known, and I seem to recall a time when you were wont to share your thoughts with me. Has so much changed?"

"Only the things I think about."

"No more ploys to trick Headmistress or fears about Latin exams? Well, what was it you came to think about?"

"I seem to recall a time when you could read my thoughts," she countered.

"Ah, but it was easy then, for I'd been a child myself and you were such a minx I had merely to recall how I'd acted when I was ten or eleven to know what you were thinking. Having, however, never been a female, I can't begin to imagine what nature of matters concern betrothed young ladies."

She couldn't help giggling. "You could try."

He feigned concentration. "Tell me, was it whether to start your day with breakfast in the dining room with the family or to order a private cup of chocolate in your suite?"

She gave a negative nod.

"The merits of silk tissue versus cashmere on a chilly night?"

Another shake of her head.

"I quite give up. You must tell me, for I've little patience with guessing games."

Lucy related the conversation she'd had with the Duchess of Mitford that afternoon and concluded, ''No matter what her grace said, I believe she may know something about my mother.''

''Which I venture to guess is important to you.''

''Oh, yes, indeed. Prodigiously important. You see, I don't even know her name. Of course, my father's family name was Wickham, but I don't know even that much about my mother.''

The longing in this response touched the earl, and at that moment, he wished above all else to be able to provide Lucy with a detailed history of her mother's family tree. ''There might be a connection after all between the duchess and your mother,'' he speculated. ''I seem to recollect some tale about the old duke having a niece who ran off with an American. It was his younger brother's daughter, and she'd barely finished her Season when she eloped with this fellow, and no one heard of either of them again.''

''He wasn't a ship's captain, was he?''

''I've no idea, and what little I do know isn't firsthand,'' he cautioned. ''I was only a small boy when I heard my mother and her friends whispering over tea. Quite a scandal for hereabouts. Her name was Lillabet. And even if they hadn't disappeared, I don't believe Lady Lillabet and her husband would have been welcomed at Aylesbury, for the duke and his brother never approved of this American, or so my mother and her friends claimed.''

''Did Lady Bronwen know Lady Lillabet?''

''At least a nodding acquaintance, I should think. I'll tell you what—''

''Yes?'' she interrupted in eagerness.

''I shall do what I can to assist you in finding out about your parents,'' he promised, liking the notion that there was something he could do for Lucy, something which Dalsany had apparently neglected to do, and liking even more the notion that he would have a legitimate reason to seek out her company. "I shall leave the duchess to you, but shall on my own make a few discreet inquiries."

"That's very generous of you."

"Not at all," he mumbled, wishing that he might do much more, particularly something to prevent the misery she was bound to experience as Dalsany's bride. It was pointless, however, to think of such a thing, for he knew a young person in love would never believe the truth, and as long as Lucy loved Dalsany he would not be the one to destroy her pretty fantasy. Such revelations would have to be discovered on her own, and as he'd told his mother, when that occurred he'd be at the ready to help her in any way necessary.

"Christ's nails!" a voice cried out behind them. It was Dalsany, running toward them with a mixture of confusion and panic upon his countenance. His eyes darted from Lucy to his uncle, sitting on the ground, the pair of them covered with dirt and far too close for comfort. "What in God's name is going on here?" he demanded.

"Your uncle saved me." Lucy looked toward the spot where the ground had fallen away, a line of dark moist dirt marking the break in the cliff. "I would have fallen to my death if he hadn't come along to save me."

Somewhat pacified by this explanation he calmed down a bit, but still cast a wary eye upon his uncle. The earl's expression was once again grim. There was no sign that he had smiled and laughed with Lucy, and when he spoke his voice was as hard as it had been that first night at dinner. "And now, Anthony, it's your turn to rescue me. It's a good thing you've come along. I wasn't sure I was going to be able to get up myself, and I certainly couldn't have called upon Miss Wickham."

Dalsany assisted Lucy, then gave his uncle a hand. "You're all right, aren't you?" he asked Lucy.

"Yes, just frightened."

"I'm sure she could do with a hot bath and some pampering," injected the earl. "Take her back to the house, Anthony, and see that she gets tea and make sure the maid sets a good fire in her rooms."

"But what about you?" Lucy turned back to the earl, who was leaning upon his cane. She feared he was in pain and she thought that of the two of them he needed more pampering than herself, but her expression revealed a far different emotion, and the earl read it well. *Do we tell Dalsany? Or are we still the earl and Miss Wickham?* was her silent question.

"I'm all right, Miss Wickham." His clipped response told her all she needed to know. "Please go on. I believe I'd like to watch the sun set," he said in such a way that it was more of a dismissal than anything else.

Dalsany led Lucy back toward Clovelly. At the top of the crest she looked back and saw Pip's tall lonely figure slowly making its way westward, and a flood of tears streamed down her face.

"Delayed reaction to the shock," consoled the viscount. He wrapped an arm about her shoulders and led her into the marble rotunda, where Lady Bronwen and the twins crowded about to offer comfort and to hear about the accident.

"Where's Uncle Alex now?" This came from

Edith, who upon learning he was still on the cliff dashed through the French doors and across the lawn while Lady Bronwen and Eglantine fussed over Lucy. A special drink of warmed milk with a touch of whiskey and honey was ordered, a hot bath was drawn in the brass tub in her dressing room, and Lady Bronwen herself, suspecting that something far more momentous than a narrow escape from a cliff fall had transpired that evening, stayed by Lucy until the girl who would be the next Countess of Harrow drifted to sleep.

That Sunday the first reading of the banns was carried out at St. Catherine's Chapel in Fleet Regis. It was also the Sunday for the annual spring fair, and following the Eucharist everyone filed down Water Street to the nearby field, where girls and boys decorated the maypole with flower crowns and ribbons and streamers. Fleet Regis wasn't a large town, really nothing more than a fishing village with two dirt thoroughfares that intersected at the old Norman chapel, and on this particular Sunday both High and Water streets were clogged with colorful booths of itinerant merchants.

Over the past centuries the ancient custom of celebrating the coming of spring had evolved. The pagan rituals of Mayday were no longer performed in Fleet Regis, but the populace still seized any excuse to dance and sing and enjoy themselves, and the annual spring fair provided that opportunity. Water Street ran parallel to the Fleet—a narrow sea loch between the coast and a seven-mile bank of pebbles with a reputation for shipwreck, smugglers, mackerel, and dangerous currents—and it ended in an open field, where on this day of general jollification a hodgepodge of tents, roundabouts and swings was clustered about the maypole.

"What are you doing alone?" the earl asked Lucy when he discovered her wandering through the churchyard. She was dressed in spring green, a color he thought most becoming. It matched her deep green eyes and put him in mind of an apple blossom just before it flowered.

"You mother is in consultation with Lady Asquith and the Reverend," she replied with a smile, for she found she was glad to see him. They hadn't had a chance to visit alone since those moments on the cliff, but when she sat at his right side at the twelve-foot dining room table or when they passed on the terrace or in the rotunda, his expression always gentled and she knew he was sharing a secret private hello with her. She wanted to tell him she had missed him, but even Lucy knew that was highly inappropriate, so she merely explained about his mother. "The ladies are discussing something about a repair fund for the church roof."

"And Anthony?" He fell into step beside her. The ground was level and the grass well trimmed, and he had no trouble keeping pace with her.

"He went off with Edith, who was pleading for a spin on one of the roundabouts." She didn't mention that Eglantine had gone off in search of the organist, Mr. Pratt, for she didn't wish to get the dark-haired girl in trouble with Lady Bronwen. Contrary to what Edith had claimed the bespectacled Mr. Pratt seemed a rather benign fellow who was likely more in danger of being bored to tears by Eglantine than himself posing any threat to the girl's reputation.

"Rather rude to leave you to your own devices," he remarked.

"I don't mind." Lucy paused before a lichen-covered grave slab and bent down to flick off several pieces of moss. From the nearby field a chorus of children's voices rose in song: *Here we go 'round the merry maypole, the merry maypole, the merry maypole.* Lucy glanced over her shoulder to see the hand-clasped youngsters circling the wreathed pole.

"You didn't wish to explore the fair?"

"I was looking for a clue to Lady Lillibet. If her family is from Dorset, perhaps I might find a clue. Someone with the same name. Mayhap there's even an obscure, long-forgotten Wickham buried here."

"I think the Duchess of Mitford is a far more likely source of intelligence than old grave slabs," he opined kindly.

"But I didn't see her in church. Perhaps she's not well."

"Old gel has her own chapel. Hasn't worshiped with the rest of us since the duke died. Except for Easter and Christmas of course."

"Then there must be—"

"Yes, there's a Mitford memorial temple at Aylesbury. They're all interred there," he finished her sentence for her, having known what she was thinking before she'd uttered the words. "Quite overdone actually. Rather like the Parthenon on the outside and on the inside there are rows of black marble urns. You'll see it all when you go to tea, I'm sure. Aylesbury is quite a showplace. The old king often dined there when he was at Weymouth, and there's a suite named in his honor."

They exited the churchyard and strolled to a tent where refreshments were being served. There were apple slices dipped in green whipped cream

and green peppermint ice, and Lucy tasted everything, including a Jack-in-the-Bush, a giant gin-
gerbread man wearing a May wreath of parsley
upon his head.

Behind them a cacophony of shrieks pierced the
air, and Lucy turned to see Edith and Dalsany
riding one of the roundabouts. The contraption
seemed to rotate with breakneck speed and the
riders screamed anew.

"My goodness," Lucy gasped in fascination.

"Have you ever ridden one?"

"No."

"Come along then." He took her hand in his,
but she didn't move. His voice came soft as velvet, and he tempted Lucy. "Let yourself be free
again, Minx."

The earl's teasing words had the desired effect,
causing Lucy's heart to flip-flop at his reference
to the past, and a hint of high color to touch her
cheeks. She was sorry that she might have
changed so much that he did not like her, she was
alarmed that she cared so much for his approbation, and she experienced a prick of challenge to
prove that she was still herself. This troubled her,
and she wished that she might be able to make
precise sense of her emotions. Responding with a
tentative smile, for she was at once as wary of the
mechanical contraption as she was of her reaction to the earl, Lucy held his hand as they
crossed the field to another roundabout, where an
attendant seated them side by side in a small
bucket-shaped seat.

Slowly, the machine cranked into action, several of the other riders oohed and aahed, and the
wooden seat began to swing from side to side. A
funny little nervous sensation beset Lucy. She
rather wished to be standing upon the ground in-

stead of dangling from the air, and closing her
eyes, she clasped her hands upon her lap as the
roundabout picked up speed. Then the roundabout gave a wild jolt to one side, the earl's hand
fell over hers, and in that instant, it didn't matter
anymore whether Lucy wished to be seated there
or not.

Something coursed though her, her eyes
opened wide, and she experienced a rush of ter-
rifying pleasure that was heightened by the rock-
ing movement of the roundabout. She was giddy
and light-headed, and she made no effort to resist
when the earl pulled her closer into his embrace
allowing their legs to touch, thigh to thigh.

The machine went faster, Lucy cried out and
clung to him, and his blood quickened. Faster yet
twirled the roundabout, and Lucy's straw bonnet
fell off, wisps of pale blond hair whipped about
her face, her eyes sparkled with exhilaration, and
a delightful pink touched her cheeks. She looked
like an angel, young and fresh and sweet, and
when she smiled up at him, the earl wanted nothing more than to bend down and allow his mouth
to taste those pretty lips. The temptation was
strong, and he closed his eyes against it, but the
desire remained. Lucy laughed and whispered in
his ear. "Oh, I do thank you, Pip, ever so much.
I shall never forget this." And acutely aware of
her warmth and softness, the earl knew that if he
were a less experienced gentleman, his heart—as
his mother had suggested—might be in serious
danger.

"I've never done anything like this before.
Never." Lucy exclaimed, her eyes sparkling.

The earl, despite his best intentions, laced his
fingers through Lucy's where his hand rested

lightly upon hers, his blue gaze warmly enveloping her.

All the surrounding brouhaha and activity faded away, and Lucy thought this must be what it was like to be cocooned in a whirlpool. Her senses were aware of Pip and nothing more, and an unfamiliar melting sensation uncoiled within Lucy until her stomach knotted with expectation. She held her breath and swallowed hard, for she knew this was the sort of moment when the gentleman in a romantic drama kissed the heroine. Lucy waited, feeling both hot and cold, almost as if she'd fallen victim to a sudden fever, but Pip didn't kiss her, and when she exhaled that pent-up breath a single tear welled forth from her eye to trail down her cheek.

"There must be something in my eye," she whispered, averting her gaze and searching through her reticule for a handkerchief. It was wrong to feel this way. Wrong to have fancied that Pip might kiss her, wrong to be so disappointed, and another tear escaped to trail after the other, this time largely owing to guilt and fear.

"Dust, I suspect." Gently, he tilted her head to inspect her eye. There was nothing there, but his hand lingered upon her face. Her skin was deliciously soft, it invited caressing, and he allowed his thumb to trace a tiny circle at the corner of her eye.

Sweet Lord, but it invited more than caressing, and though he knew it was sheer folly, he did the unthinkable. He kissed the corner of her eye. Briefly, softly, sweetly. Nothing more, yet it was still folly, and he swallowed hard in order to say, "Whatever it was, it's all gone now. You'll be fine."

Fine. Her eyes began to tear again. Her skin was

warm where his lips had all too quickly rested. *Fine?* It was all well and good to say everything was going to be fine, but she knew otherwise. She knew that was impossible, and she couldn't dismiss the foreboding that in her haste to go out into the world and establish a family of her own she had made a terrible terrible mistake.

Nine
❦❦❦❦

TEA AT AYLESBURY was a horrendous disappointment. Lucy arrived at the appointed time in the company of Lady Bronwen—Dalsany having opted instead to accompany his sisters on a pony cart ride to the Fox Strangways estate, and the earl being once again in consultation with his estate manager. The ladies were shown into a humid and ill-tended conservatory only to be received by her grace's companion, Miss Elizabeth Somerville-Large, a penniless distaff relative from Dublin, who appeared more interested in sorting embroidery yarn than receiving visitors.

"Her grace is napping," Miss Somerville-Large stated without preface. "Your appointment must have slipped her mind, for she did not mention it to me at all. You know how forgetful the elderly can be," she intoned in a haughty tenor as if she herself weren't approaching her seventh decade.

The subsequent tea was perfunctory and proper, conversation was limited to the unusually favorable weather and the latest efforts to raise funds to refurbish the chapel roof in Fleet Regis. There was no mention of Lucy's antecedents, nor any reference to her resemblance to anyone whatsoever; there was no tour of Aylesbury and its

113

grounds, nor glimpse into the King William Room, and after the requisite time had elapsed Lucy and Lady Bronwen made their farewells.

"Enow, Lucy, it was a disappointment, I know," consoled Lady Bronwen on their return journey to Clovelly. She gave Lucy's hand a comforting squeeze.

"I was fully prepared not to learn a thing," replied Lucy. She lifted her chin in a fortifying sort of pose.

The older woman studied the young girl beside her. Having herself been of no help when Lucy had inquired about Lady Lillibet, the dowager countess had been aware of how important this interview at Aylesbury was for Lucy. The girl had confided in her, had shown her the pretty gold locket and told of her pledge to fill it with pictures, and now seeing how ably Lucy put on a brave face, Lady Bronwen was disturbed. The child had had much practice with such behavior, it appeared. What a tragedy, for she deserved much more happiness than that, much more happiness, she was loath to admit, than she would ever find with Dalsany.

"I'm sure there shall be another time to visit with her grace, and even if there weren't, you must not worry, for we don't care one way or the other. Your parentage doesn't matter to us. I am vastly satisfied that Anthony has found a young lady as nice as yourself. That's all that counts. Except, of course, that you fit into our family. You do feel at home at Clovelly, don't you?"

"Yes, ma'am, you've made me most welcomed. Every one of you," was Lucy's sincere but lackluster reply.

"Still you wish to know of your mama. I can understand, for I lost a child once. A little lassie.

Although there was nothing to know, for the wee thing lived less than twelve days, even now after so many years I can't help thinking what might have been. Would she have had a good seat on a horse? Or would she have preferred watercolors and lessons on the pianoforte? Would she have looked like Eglantine or, perhaps, more like Edith? It's not knowing the answers that's most haunting. Am I correct?''

''Oh, ma'am, you do understand. If I only knew then I would be satisfied. How did you know?''

Lady Bronwen gave Lucy's forearm another reassuring pat. ''We're both women, are we not? You must never hesitate to talk with me about anything.''

The carriage came to a stop at the bottom of the horseshoe staircase. The earl, dark and splendid as a pirate king, was standing on the bottom step, and Lucy's spirits lifted and a smile radiated her face for the first time since she'd entered the conservatory at Aylesbury. Lady Bronwen took note of this reaction and her brows knitted together in a speculative frown. Again, she wondered what had happened that night on the cliff. Had Lucy and her son been reunited? And if that were the case, what were the girl's true feelings for Alex? As fond as she was of Dalsany, she couldn't help wishing that Lucy might love her son instead of her nephew. Anthony was clever and amusing, but he didn't have a heart; Alex, however, did, and thus it was that the dowager countess, who had theretofore never meddled in other people's affairs, found herself considering how she might open Miss Wickham's eyes, and bring joy to her son while still managing to save her nephew from the duns.

Of a sudden, she exclaimed to Lucy, "How silly of me to have forgotten, I promised Ned Claggett in the stables that I'd visit the yard to see the new foal. Bathsheba's colt came late last night. You need not tag along, my dear. Go on into the house and enjoy a little rest before dinner." With that she shooed Lucy from the landau and ordered the groom to drive on to the stables.

"Hello, Lucy." The earl gave a nod. His expression gentled as the carriage wheeled away. "My mother?"

"She wished to see Bathsheba's foal."

"And you have no interest in horseflesh."

"I do, but"—She caught herself and stopped mid-sentence. Twin spots of crimson rose upon her cheeks. She had been about to state the obvious: *Your mother seemed intent upon leaving me in your company.* Such an admission, however, was both peculiar and provocative and was best left unsaid. Instead, she merely said, "I was tired."

"Ah, then it was an exhausting interview with her grace." He offered his arm to escort her up the stairs. She accepted. "Profitable, too, I trust."

Before Lucy might tell him what had happened the twins' pony cart, Dalsany holding the ribbons, came careening down the drive. The girls called out a duet of exuberant hallos as the viscount brought the vehicle to a halt at the foot of the horseshoe stairs. Dalsany handed the reins to a stable boy, who had appeared out of nowhere, and without offering assistance to either of his sisters, he bounded from his seat and hurried to Lucy's side.

"Hallo, Lucy. Did the sleuthing pay off?" He dropped a proprietary kiss upon Lucy's forehead and wrapping an arm about her waist drew her away from his uncle.

"No," she replied, experiencing a most unexpected reluctance to confide in Dalsany.

"Then perhaps this will be the end of it," was his inept retort, a trail of impatience in his voice. "Can't have you moping about with a wedding on the horizon. Not the thing, you know. You ought to be celebrating. By the by, you ought to spend some time with Lady Priscilla. She's a particularly talented young lady, you know. Showed me her watercolors. She does know how to amuse herself, I must say."

That Dalsany owned not one ounce of empathy for Lucy was apparent, and the earl knew an almost irrepressible urge to thrash his nephew for such gross insensitivity. While he managed to look away from the younger gentleman without revealing his disfavor for him, the earl did something far more revealing than anything he could have said. Before he might stop himself, he cupped his hand beneath Lucy's elbow and gently pulled her toward him, away from the viscount.

Lucy's great green eyes widened, and her gaze narrowed to read the earl's expression, and what she saw etched upon his stormy male features discomposed her further. That open display of protectiveness—nay, almost possessiveness—caused her heart to somersault. Yet in the next moment it vanished, that somber facade prevailed, and her heart contracted with what seemed a pang of disappointment. Perhaps it had been nothing more than a trick of the late afternoon light or her own confused state of mind.

Deporting oneself like a proper young lady was taxing in the extreme, particularly when a young lady owned an excess of worries. Lucy knew it was improper to slip out of the house and even more scandalous to contemplate a midnight swim. She could hear Headmistress: "Now, Lucy, if the good Lord had wished young ladies to swim he would have endowed you with a fair-frilled pair of gills, and I, in turn, would have seen that appropriate instruction was added to your curriculum. Public exposure to water is not, however, an acceptable activity for young ladies. You are never to set foot in the ocean again," she had concluded this annual lecture in stern admonishment.

Lucy had always answered Headmistress with a polite "Yes, ma'am," accompanied by a dutiful curtsy, her fingers during all of this being, however, crossed behind her back. It wasn't that Lucy was dishonest precisely, rather that with so few pleasures to call her own there was simply no way she would give up her outings to the beach. Matters had changed very little. Lucy still thought of swimming as something special, and no matter what anyone said or how other things might change, she could always swim. So it was that despite the bounds of propriety Lucy found herself standing on the top step of the pool wearing nothing more than a muslin nightgown.

Headmistress wasn't the only one talking to her from the past. There was also a deep male voice.

"All the females in my family know how to swim," Pip had told her when he'd held her hand and led her face-on into the surf. "My grandfather started our rather odd family tradition when he taught his wife and daughters. Expands the chest and promotes digestion, he claimed. Plus encourages self-reliance, a quality all too lacking in the gentler sex. In turn, my father taught his wife and children." The waves had crashed about him, and they'd both jumped as the water broke over their shoulders. She laughed and he joined in her unbridled merriment. "Mind you, my mother doesn't cavort on Chesil Beach in this fashion, but she would be the first to acclaim the virtues of swimming. To breast the waves is as exhilarating to the spirit as clearing a five-barred gate on horseback. Does wonders for reviving the body and soul."

With that in mind, Lucy descended the tile steps, and when she stood waist-deep, she cupped her hands to scoop up the water and toss it over her shoulders. She shivered. It was chilly, and she lowered herself in a single motion up to her neck, then she submerged herself and swam several yards beneath the water before surfacing to sit upon a bottom step at the opposite side. There was something matchless about swimming that caused her to smile as she tilted back her head, curls of pale hair fanning out about her like a cloud of sea kelp; as if liberated from her earthly self, she floated upon the water, and in that blissful moment, she was able to escape. She didn't care if the Duchess of Mitford knew her mother, she didn't care what the earl thought of her or why she was so confused whenever he was around, nor did she care if she wed Anthony and stayed at Clovelly and ever had the family for which she had always yearned.

At length, she opened her eyes. Fingers of moonlight streaked through the Doric-columned windows of the circular building. A fresco on the domed ceiling overhead was illuminated, and Lucy stared at Poseidon the sea king, his beard flowing in the wind, a trident in his hand, and driving a golden chariot upon the crest of a great foaming wave. Her thoughts drifted as she imagined what it might be like to live as a sea goddess or at the very least a winged water baby or sea otter. It couldn't help but be a most idyllic existence, she decided with a sigh.

A sound in the water drew her from this reverie, and turning from her back to her side, she emitted a high-pitched gasp. There was a man standing no more than a foot or two away from her, and she found herself eye level with a bare and very male chest.

"Don't be alarmed," the gentleman said from his corner.

The masculine voice was deep and warm, and Lucy knew it well.

"Is that you, Pip?" she asked on a nervous giggle. That the gentleman in the corner was her old friend and not some stranger offered little comfort to Lucy. His presence was far too unsettling. She didn't understand her feelings, and in particular, why her confidence in the future was no longer as positive as when she'd agreed to marry the viscount. Lucy had never been one to worry, but that seemed to have changed, and the more time she spent around the earl, the more doubts she had about herself and the future. Something wasn't right, and she didn't think spending more time around the earl was going to help her find answers.

"Yes, just me," he replied in a somewhat penitent tone, for he owned more than a twinge of shame that he hadn't made his presence known to Lucy when she first entered the bathing grotto. That would have been the proper and gentlemanly course, but when she'd taken off her dressing gown and the moon had bathed her enticing female form in silver light, he'd been unable to resist watching her from his darkened corner. The outline of her breasts and long shapely legs barely visible through the sheer fabric of her nightgown was tantalizing, but more than that the simple sight of her gliding through the water had been a catharsis to his soul. For several minutes, he'd remained upon the step, savoring an altogether rare contentment. This glimpse of Lucy was like a sparkling elixir, and although he had no rights where she was concerned, he couldn't deny himself this pleasure, nor could he resist speaking.

"This is much more like you. Rather confirms my faith in the world to see you sneaking off for a swim."

"Are you mocking me?"

"Quite to the contrary. It's a compliment."

If he had hoped to please her, this remark did the opposite. Lucy's heart contracted with despair. "Am I that much changed?"

"No. Merely grown up into a proper young lady. If I hadn't known you before, I'd never suspect there was a freer spirit within your heart and soul."

Her lower lip trembled. What did he know of her heart? She lifted her chin in a sort of defense. "I am affianced to your nephew and heir. Surely I owe Dalsany and your family a certain measure of decorum."

"Ah, true, but were you betrothed to me I wouldn't allow that spirit to fade away, rather I should cultivate it," he was so bold to say.

Hot tears pricked Lucy's eyes. He wasn't being intentionally cruel, she told herself, and while she wished to offer some rebuttal in Dalsany's favor, if not her own, she was robbed of the ability to speak.

In a voice that fell as soft as velvet, he went on. "I would let you run barefoot on the sand . . .

walk without a hat in the mist . . . and I would hold you in my arms when you wished to stand upon a rock while the ocean crashed about you." A seductive quality laced his final words: "I would let you dare while I kept you safe."

He heard her intake of breath, saw her eyes widen, and he thought he detected a trembling in her lower lip. A knot tightened in his chest. He hadn't meant to upset her, and he reached out to brush an errant lock of hair from her forehead.

A gasp escaped her when his fingers brushed against her brow. His words were bad enough, but his tender touch would be her ruination, and doing the first thing that came to mind, Lucy ducked beneath the water and held her breath for as long as she could before resurfacing several feet away from him.

"You must not touch me," was her urgent whisper.

To which there was nothing he could say. He couldn't lie and claim his intentions had been innocent, nor could he say anything that might compromise her any more than the impropriety of the situation already had. In the distance, the surf rumbled against the coast, the plaintive song of a thrush drifted on the night air, and the sound of their breathing seemed oddly magnified in the cavernous grotto.

At length, he offered an attempt to break the silence.

"It's my exercise. I come for my exercise."

"Yes, I've heard that water is a great restorative." Grateful for this unexceptional line of discourse, Lucy managed a smile that was reflected in her voice as it drifted across the water, clear and light and rather like the music of a pretty bell floating through the darkness.

The earl responded with a smile of his own. Almost all of his pain was gone. "That's what my doctor tells me. Although I have often questioned his credentials. Sometimes I think the gentleman is better trained for the task of examiner in the Inquisition than the healing profession."

"I've always had a loathing for physicians myself," she confided.

"I know," he said.

"Pray, don't tell me you still remember that time I cut my foot on the mussel shell and fainted?"

"It would be rather impossible to forget," he teased, his mind's eye seeing her child's form collapsed upon the sand, her outstretched leg covered with blood. The injury had looked far worse than it had been, although two stitches had been required, and Lucy had been more upset with her cowardice at having fainted than with the tiny scar. "Don't worry, I shall never allow you to meet Dr. Parke. The fellow owns the most deplorable fondness for the saw. He never thought I'd make it this far without his services, but I rather showed him otherwise. Though it hasn't been easy."

Lucy didn't know that she had drawn from the earl in a few moments more than most men had in months. Her heart swelled with compassion at what he must have endured, and the soft inflection in her voice turned her next words into a question rather than a statement.

"Your leg pains you?"

"On occasion," he replied in a matter-of-fact tone that didn't reveal his astonishment at the extent of what he'd said to Lucy.

Neither did his voice hint at the extent of his current affliction. Foolishly, he'd overused his leg this morning when he and Edith had moved Captain Pomeroy to the closed north wing of Clovelly. Sir Denis Flyte had organized a cliff patrol. Their intentions were noble, but even Sir Denis wasn't above suspicion, and fearing Captain Pomeroy's discovery, the earl and Edith had moved the wounded man from the cottage and up three flights of stairs. The subsequent throbbing in his knee joint was so excruciating he'd been unable to leave his study for the remainder of the day, nor had he recovered by dinner to join the family. In fact, he'd been at the plunge pool since dusk and had imbibed rather liberally from a silver flask that now lay empty on the terra-cotta floor.

"Believe it has something to do with weightlessness. Floating in the water, that is. Relieves the pressure," he remarked, rather intrigued by the sight of Lucy staring at his bare chest and wishing that he might see her precise expression. Was she blushing? Was she mortified? Or was she, he dared to speculate, in the least bit intrigued?

In point of fact, the earl's bare chest fascinated Lucy. Long ago, she'd seen Pip divested of jacket and shirt, naked from the waist up and ready to enter the ocean, but somehow her memory hadn't fully recorded an image of the corded muscles that ran across his stomach. Now she couldn't stop herself staring. An odd inward tremor skirled through Lucy, and she forced her gaze upward to his face.

"You're not wearing your eye patch!" She could hardly believe she hadn't noticed that fact until this moment, and she risked floating closer for a better look. "There's nothing wrong with your eye either. Is there?"

"No, there's nothing wrong," he admitted in reference to his eye, but feeling, on the other hand, there was quite a bit wrong with the way she was bobbing about him. Egad, why wouldn't the chit stay still? He hadn't meant to tell the truth about his eye, but he couldn't think clearly while she hovered so near.

"Well, why in heaven's name are you wearing that thing?"

"It's part of a ruse." He hesitated, giving himself time to stop thinking about the way she was churning up the water between his thighs. Combined with the effects of the brandy, this motion was producing a potent effect upon him, and he feared he might loose control of his good intentions.

"A ruse?" she prompted, whereupon he regained the strength to focus on their conversation.

Although his military training had drilled into him that anyone could be a double agent, his instinct told him to trust Lucy. He lowered his voice; sound carried over water, and one could never be too cautious. "I'm working for the Foreign Office, you see, and we thought the more crippled I appeared the less noticed my activities might be. We didn't want anyone to think I posed a threat to the individual we're searching for."

Her response was an outbreak of uncontrolled laughter.

"This is extremely serious business, you know. We have it on highly reputable authority there's an Englishman in the vicinity who knows the full details of a dangerous plot to assassinate Field Marshal Wellington abroad and Lord Liverpool at home."

"I don't doubt the seriousness of this, not for

an instant, and you must pardon me my amusement," she managed as her giggles subsided. "It's just that there's nothing inconspicuous about you in the least. Oh, Pip, if you only could see yourself. That eye patch doesn't make you look harmless. You're quite ferocious, in fact. And far too masculine. Even with the cane and the patch you're a powerful figure of a man." Exceedingly thankful for the cover of darkness, she felt a furious blush burn her face. She changed the subject. "And your visits with the estate manager? Can I assume that in actuality you've been off and about on this Foreign Office business?" He replied in the affirmative, and she went on. "Does anyone else know about this?"

"Edith."

She hadn't expected this. "What? How could you endanger her like that?"

"I had little choice. She discovered one of my agents on the beach, and she's been helping me care for him since. It seemed the best way to guarantee her discretion, and I did need her assistance. Although the patch is a ruse, the cane isn't."

"Well, now that I know can I help?"

"Perhaps. I'm sure Edith could use an extra hand." In the next moment, he changed his mind. "I don't like the notion of putting you in danger."

"Why me and not Edith?"

"No one gives Edith a second thought when she wanders off for hours. She's always loved to walk the cliffs by herself. But as for you, people would notice."

"Well, I suppose you're right. I am new and rather a curiosity."

"No, that's not what I mean. Didn't you know?

A beautiful woman is always noticed,'' he said, his voice catching on a husky whisper.

A sharp little pain pierced Lucy's heart. Oh, how she wished that Dalsany might say such things to her. While the viscount had seemed almost perfect in London, now she found herself considering that she might want something more of the man she would marry. It was a selfish and altogether sobering thought. She'd no right to criticize Anthony; after all, he cared enough to make her his wife and that alone should have told Lucy everything she needed to know about him as a gentleman and future husband. She'd no right to be so pleased with the way the earl was watching her.

A shaft of moonlight revealed his intense regard, and Lucy felt like a doe, unable to turn away from the hunter's scrutiny. A shiver worked its way up her spine.

''My God, you're trembling. You must be freezing,'' he exclaimed as he stood, reached behind him, and produced a large linen wrapper. He held it open for her. ''Come on. Let me dry you off.'' Lucy stared as if dumbstruck, whereupon he encouraged, ''I won't eat you alive. I'm perfectly harmless.''

But there was nothing reassuring about the silky way he spoke, nothing harmless about the way her heart leapt when he drew her from the pool, wrapped the cloth about her, and began to rub her arms and shoulders. Her knees weakened, and suddenly aware of his warm breath against the nape of her neck, her trembling began anew. Abruptly, she pushed away from him.

''Thank you. It's gotten very late. Too late,'' she babbled. ''I must return.''

He sighed and bid her a reluctant farewell.

"Ah, then, I must bid you good evening." As if playing at a dangerous game, he'd knowingly overstepped the bounds. It was a good thing she was leaving before it was too late, and he let her depart without delay. Still he couldn't resist another peak at Lucy when she went through the arched door and down the moonlit cobbled path toward the house. He saw the curve of her hips and swell of her breasts, and experiencing a renewal of his earlier arousal, he knew that under different circumstances she wouldn't have been safe with him in the grotto. He had wanted to ask her about Dalsany, and if she truly loved the younger man. Hell, he wanted to make love to her, and were it not for the betrothal, he would never have let her leave without holding her in his arms and kissing her until the melding of their lips gave way to a fullness of passion that would have marked her as his for all time.

Usually, the earl slept soundly after a dip in the plunge pool, but he knew that this night he would pass several sleepless hours besieged by images of Lucy. Lucy on the roundabout. Lucy in the plunge pool. Lucy laughing, smiling. Lucy concerned and selfless and thinking of everyone else before herself. Lucy of the great green eyes and golden curls and luscious figure. Lucy the delightful child who had grown up to be an exceedingly desirable young woman.

His mother was right. This wasn't going to turn out with a simple happily-ever-after ending.

"I believe there were poachers in the park last night." Dalsany offered this casual observation between his fifth and sixth mouthfuls of kippers.

Across the table, Edith froze in panic and she felt the awful sensation of her stomach plummeting to the floor. Was it spies? Had someone seen her and Uncle Alex move Captain Pomeroy? Was Clovelly being watched? The anxious girl glanced toward her uncle, but his expression did not reveal the slightest concern, and with a sigh of relief she resumed rolling a boiled egg into her serviette. She needed to return to Captain Pomeroy as soon as possible. His appetite was gargantuan these days, which meant she was going to have to visit several times a day while he was in the north wing.

Although it was early, barely half past eight, the entire household was gathered in the dining room. Cook had outdone herself this morning with an array of dishes, and Lady Bronwen insisted that they eat heartily, for the ladies had a formidable social schedule ahead of them for which Belgian chocolate and dry toast would not provide sufficient nourishment. No less than six invitations for informal visits had been delivered from nearby estates plus two from summer residents in Weymouth, and Lady Bronwen, in consultation with the head groom, had devised an itinerary that would cover some thirty-two miles and allow them to pay a brief call upon each of those six neighbors. They would depart Clovelly promptly at quarter past nine o'clock, and traveling in the comfort of Lady Bronwen's landau, they would not return until dusk.

"Must I go, Grandmother?" Edith inquired.

"Why ever not? You always love a carriage ride, and rigorous though this particular jaunt may prove to be, etiquette demands we accept every single one of these invitations. Dorset must get to know our dear Lucy as soon as possible."

"But I feel a megrim coming on," the girl pleaded, her pallor lending credence to this fabrication. She loathed duplicity, but she had no choice. Having promised to read to Captain Pomeroy, nothing must keep her from that duty. Truth to tell, duty had very little to do with her concern for the captain. It was love, she was certain of it. What else would account for the breathlessness she experienced each time she visited the captain and he looked up to bid her hello? What else would account for the fact that her head was so filled with thoughts of Captain Pomeroy that she could neither sleep nor eat and had lost all interest in her shell collection and watching for chicks at the rook hatchery on the cliff?

Lady Bronwen frowned. ''We would not want you ill for the gala ball, would we? It will be your and Eglantine's first formal occasion in public, so just this once I suppose you may remain behind. But you must promise to rest.''

''Yes, ma'am. Of course, I shall not leave the house.'' Some color returned to Edith's cheeks as she slipped the wrapped egg into her pinafore pocket. Perhaps, she fancied, this spy business would be over in a day or two, and Captain Pomeroy would be able to attend the ball. Then wouldn't Eglantine be surprised to discover she had a beau who was even more handsome than the organist, Mr. Pratt?

''Back to the issue of poachers,'' injected Dalsany.

''Poachers?'' The earl raised his ink-black eyebrows. Although he didn't smile, there was something distinctly amused about his expression. ''Rather early in the season, don't you think?''

''While I barely glimpsed it, I've no doubt there was some sort of movement near the bathing grotto.''

Lucy, who had been holding her breath ever since the viscount's initial mention of poachers in the wood, wondered if the earl would admit to having been to the plunge pool. She turned her head toward him; their gazes met and held for the space of several heartbeats.

"Can't imagine what it was," the earl drawled, his intense sea blue regard never wavering from Lucy.

Lucy exhaled. It was another secret between them, but this time acknowledged. A shared secret that was more than a little scandalous. They had been at the plunge pool together, at night, barely clothed and without a chaperone, and Lucy became aware of a sudden heat rising upon her face. There was something decidedly wicked about sharing such a past, and the earl's intense gaze told her his mind was entertaining similar thoughts. There was no denying his sensual underlook. The dots of color upon her cheeks heightened to a dramatic crimson.

She was blushing, and the earl liked the notion that he had that effect on her. He liked it very much. The image of her tantalizing silhouette in the moonlit doorway was still fresh upon his mind, and the bright red tint upon her complexion was proof that she was not immune to him. That he affected her in this way was a most invigorating development to consider. A burst of energy seemed to flow through him, and for the first time in ages, he could believe good things were possible. It was almost as if he were whole again. He couldn't explain the how or why of what was happening to him. All that mattered was it was real; it wasn't an afternoon's fantasy or another dream from which he would soon awaken.

"Poachers. Well, I suppose that's possible," the earl conceded.

"Or smugglers," the viscount suggested.

"Or a Frenchie spy." This from Eglantine in her usual tone of high drama.

Whereupon Lady Bronwen switched the subject to talk of the gala she was planning in honor of the betrothed couple. "It shall be in two weeks. Just before the final reading of the banns at St. Catherine's. I've drawn up an invitation list and the kitchen staff is already preparing pastries, but you must tell me how elaborate you would like this to be. Mayhap, Lucy, you would like a masked ball?"

"I think a masked ball would be vastly amusing, Mother," said the earl. "And I'm sure Lucy would appreciate the attendant preparation for such a spectacle."

"Yes, I think I'd like that, ma'am. Thank you for suggesting it."

"Don't tell me *you* plan to attend!" Dalsany exclaimed. As if this remark weren't totally lacking in tact, he pointed a forkful of kippers at the earl.

An awkward silence fell over the room, then to the amazement of everyone assembled at the breakfast table, the earl said, "Attend the ball? Indeed, I might do just that."

Lucy glanced sideways at the earl. Their gazes connected and held, and although the earl maintained his customary dour facade, Lucy knew that Pip was smiling on the inside. An impish smile blossomed upon her lips, and she experienced the warmth of satisfaction that she had managed to accomplish her first goal in her new home. Quite without intent she had managed—as she had once suggested to Dalsany—to bring the earl out of his shell, and now that he was out, Lucy couldn't help thinking things weren't going to be quite the same at Clovelly.

Ten
❧ ❧ ❧ ❧

"ARE YOU FEELING BETTER THIS MORNING, Captain Pomeroy?" Lucy inquired as she set a colorful arrangement of spring flowers upon the mantel. In her other arm, she was carrying yesterday's copy of the *Times* and several pieces of correspondence the earl wished to share with the captain.

For the past two days, despite Edith's protests, Lucy had been helping the girl care for Captain Pomeroy. Fair-haired and freckled, and the youngest son of a marquis, he was an agreeable gentleman, who despite his military distinctions and numerous acts of bravery was suffering acute homesickness for his parents and younger sister. His family lived in an old Queen Anne manor house on a hill overlooking the Thames in Buckinghamshire, and he liked nothing more than to talk of his boyhood on the river. Although Lucy was more than happy to listen to him reminisce, she noticed it was Edith to whom he'd rather talk. Lucy had mentioned this to the earl, and they decided there was nothing amiss. After all, Captain Pomeroy was a gentleman and Edith wasn't yet out of the schoolroom. In fact, the earl thought it a good thing if Edith's company speeded the captain's recovery; as for Edith, whose experience with men was limited to himself and her brother, getting to know Captain Pomeroy would introduce her to the highest caliber of gentleman.

"Have you had your morning walk about the room, sir?" Lucy inquired.

"Yes, Miss Wickham, and I'm getting about much better. Thank you for the flowers. What a nice idea. You've all been very nice to me, especially Lady Edith, but it is getting rather bleak holed up inside all the time. At least at the cottage I could hear the surf."

"Actually, the flowers were Edith's idea. We went out for an early morning walk in the gardens and she cut them herself."

"Lady Edith is a most thoughtful girl." He had a very nice smile, boyish and warm and sincere.

Lucy stepped away from the mantel and studied the captain. The earl didn't see what was going on, but Lucy suspected Edith's feelings for the captain were founded in something more fragile than loyalty to the Crown, and she wondered whether the freckle-faced young captain thought of Edith as a sister or something else.

"Tell me about this costume ball that's being planned," the captain suggested as Lucy plumped up the pillow on an overstuffed chair.

She pushed the chair near a dormer and opened the window as wide as it would go. "There, you can have a bit of fresh air. How did you know about the ball?"

"Lady Edith."

"Of course, I should have guessed. And did she tell you it was in honor of my betrothal?"

"Yes, but I must say I was surprised to learn Alex was going to get married."

"He isn't," said Lucy, hoping she didn't sound too ruffled.

"Oh, pardon me, I assumed you were betrothed to Alex."

"No, to his nephew," she clarified. Good heavens, what had she said or done to make the captain think she was going to marry the earl? Feeling the onset of a blush, she turned to open two more windows. The distant crash of surf drifted up to the third floor of the north wing.

"Dalsany?" The captain crossed to the overstuffed chair and slowly eased himself into the seat.

"Do you know him?"

"Vaguely. He doesn't know about me, does he?"

"Not a word." She knew the captain was wondering why she had come to know so much about him, and why it was that the earl had trusted her. He was, however, too much of a gentleman to ask these questions, and she wasn't going to confide in him. She returned to his query about the masked ball. "The household is in a state over it. Rather a grand affair, I fear."

"You fear? Don't all young ladies long for grand affairs in their honor?"

"I well, yes, I suppose I do," she replied. The truth was she was feeling like a fraud. Here she was betrothed to Anthony, yet she was confused and ambivalent and not altogether excited about the prospect of being the center of attention at Lady Bronwen's gala.

"Have you ever heard of a groom getting cold feet?" Lucy's expression told him she didn't have a clue what he was talking about, and the captain elaborated. "It's an expression. Most grooms get a bit reluctant just before the ceremony. Nerves more than anything else, but still they wonder if they're doing the right thing, making the right match. Although I've never heard anyone suggest such a thing regarding a young lady, it is possible.''

"Yes, I suppose it is," she said, feeling somewhat comforted by the notion that she wasn't the first individual to wonder if she was marrying the right person.

"While I've never been in the situation—about to marry—and while I intend to wed for love, I'm sure I'll have my share of doubts. After all, marriage is forever, and one never knows what can happen."

The door opened. "You've a guest, Lucy," was Edith's breathless declaration as she entered the room. Of late, she'd perfected a ladylike walk and she crossed to where Lucy was standing beside the captain. "The Dowager Duchess of Mitford, red sedan chair and all. Grandmother's with her now in the oval drawing room, some creature called Somerville-Large is there, too, and you're to come straightaway." Then she looked at Captain Pomeroy, a smile of celestial proportion lighting her face. "Good morning, Captain Pomeroy. I should be happy to sit and read with you."

"Thank you, Lady Edith," he said. She picked up Walpole's *The Castle of Otranto,* and he smiled as she took up where they had stopped, for he quite adored the manner in which she read as the Princess Matilda.

In that instant, Lucy forgot about Captain Pomeroy and Edith, as well as the ball. Her mind focused on only one thing: the Dowager Duchess of Mitford was at Clovelly and asking to see her. What a promising development, she thought as she tidied her hair and smoothed the bodice of her gown. "Do I look all right?" she inquired.

"Yes, fine, Lucy, just lovely," mumbled Edith, looking up from the novel. It wasn't her intention to sound impatient, but she rather disliked interruptions when she was reading to the captain. "It's only her grace, y'know, and despite the title, she's really nothing more exciting than a batty old lady."

But Lucy didn't hear, she was already heading down the corridor toward the staircase that would lead her to the oval drawing room. Out of the north wing and into the main house she dashed, until she reached the grand double door, where she paused to pinch her cheeks for a touch of color; then she pulled back her shoulders, stood straight, and took three deep breaths to slow her rapid pace before she walked into the oval drawing room in as calm and proper a demeanor as she could achieve.

The earl and the viscount rose at Lucy's entrance, and Miss Somerville-Large—seated in a window seat to gain advantage of the morning light—looked up from her embroidery and nodded as Lucy crossed the Aubusson carpet to stand before the dowager duchess and execute her most ladylike curtsy. The tiny old woman was propped up against a mountain of silver pillows and wearing a gray mullcap, ruffed about her forehead and tied under the chin, a picture which caused Lucy to smile, for the dowager duchess presented the image of a tufted nuthatch upon her nest.

"Good morning, your grace." One of Headmistress's lectures came to mind—*Never make excuses*—and thus, Lucy merely added, "I trust I haven't kept you waiting."

The ancient gray lady waved a dismissive hand.

"You're not to worry your pretty head, my dear child. Not to worry. I understand you were in the gardens. Always did love flower arranging, m'self," she said in melancholy remembrance. "Are you good at it?"

"Passing so, I've been told."

Tea and brioches were being served, but Lucy refused any refreshment, wanting nothing but to sit beside her grace and hear whatever it was she might have to say. She claimed the empty seat by the lacquered sedan chair, and the dowager duchess responded with a frail smile.

"I regret having missed you and Lady Bronwen when you came to call the other day." Again, she raised a thin hand; this time, to motion Lucy closer. "I'm not always as clearheaded as I once was. Not always focused, I'm afraid. Seem to require more naps these days and I need to keep a diary, y'know. Must refer to it constantly. Thus when I was reminded of your visit, dear child, I decided to pay a call as soon as possible."

"Thank you, your grace."

She waved a hand. "Now, gel, you must start by telling me a bit about yourself. Where you're from, for instance. Did you go off to school? I've always had a curiosity about people, y'know."

"My fiancée is very young, your grace," Dalsany was quick to interject. "I'm sure there's nothing for her to tell that would be of the slightest interest to you."

Lucy shouldn't have been shocked by the viscount. He had made his opinion on the matter of her past quite clear. Still the harshness and condescension in his words were disconcerting, and a faint sensation of heaviness as if the sun weren't really shining hung over. This wasn't the first time Dalsany had caused her to experience this unwanted feeling, and she didn't like it one jot.

"Come now, young man. Who asked you to speak for Miss Wickham?" The dowager duchess cut Dalsany with a stare that would have sent most individuals into a veritable tizzy over the security of their social status. At length, the elderly lady turned back to Lucy. "Don't pay him any heed. Even someone as young as yourself must have a story to tell. There's nothing so fascinating to me as where we're all from and how the littlest quirks of fate can alter the course of our lives."

Lucy didn't wish to harass Dalsany, nor did she wish to be disrespectful, and in confusion, she turned toward the earl. Although he didn't smile, his expression softened, and he offered a nod of encouragement. Lucy's spirits lifted. There was something special about the way he made her feel. It was as if he were telling her she was entitled to her own decisions and whatever those decisions might be they had value because they were hers. And so, despite the viscount, she began relating a bit about her years at the academy.

"The Royal Brighton Academy, you say. Name is rather familiar. Oh, yes, now I recall. I had a niece who was asked to leave. Gel was caught cavorting in the surf," the dowager duchess explained on a warble of amusement.

Hope leapt anew in Lucy. A niece at the Royal Brighton. It couldn't have been her mother, could it? But then wouldn't Headmistress have known? Wouldn't she have noticed the similarity between herself and a former student? Perhaps not. Before retiring this evening, Lucy would write Headmistress and ask about the dowager duchess's niece. For now, she screwed up her courage to ask,

"You said I had my mother's height, your grace. Does that mean you knew my mother?"

The viscount coughed once, then a second and a third time as if attempting to disrupt this line of discourse.

The dowager duchess scowled, and her tiny voice rose in annoyance. "If you're ill, young man, take yourself off. Leave the room at once. We've no desire to contract your germs." The viscount became beet red as he uttered a pardon, and the dowager bestowed a kind smile upon Lucy. "Did I know your mother? It may be, my dear child, for you bear a strong resemblance to a young lady I once knew. Your height and the green eyes, in particular. That is why I asked about your past, and now that I hear your story it seems all the more likely there's a connection. But I'm not the one who would know for sure. The gel of whom I speak was that niece. Lillibet. She was my husband's brother's child. But she didn't live at Aylesbury. Her parents were always off on the Isle of Wight or in the Highlands—where there were some family holdings—or in Town during the Season, even made an appearance in Bath from time to time. They traveled about quite a bit in those days, and they only came to Aylesbury for Christmas or funerals, which reminds me they're all gone now," was her wistful conclusion.

"Isn't there anyone?"

"Lillibet's mother, Lady Thornton, although she doesn't live far away—she resides on a family estate at Mottistone on the Isle of Wight—I haven't seen her in more than twenty years. Not since Lillibet disappeared and my husband fought with his brother. Terrible disagreement, it was. There was an American involved, you see, and no one seemed to be able to agree about anything." Her voice faded off.

Lucy held her breath and waited to hear more. No one else spoke either, for they were all quite speechless at the prospect that Lucy might find the key to her past in their very neighborhood, and the only sound in the oval drawing room was that of the wind rustling the heavy damask curtains at the windows.

The dowager duchess's eyelids fluttered closed, still she spoke. "As young brides we were quite close, Lady Thornton and I, and over the years, I've maintained a correspondence. This evening, I shall ask Miss Somerville-Large to pen a missive in my behalf. Perhaps Lady Thornton is well enough to travel. I've no feud with her and would rather like the excitement of a visitor at Aylesbury."

"A visitor, your grace?" This came from Miss Somerville-Large. She'd been in residence at Aylesbury since the duke had died ten years before, and there had never been anyone other than herself and the dowager duchess at the dining room table, let alone an overnight guest.

"And why not, Elizabeth?" The dowager duchess opened her eyes. "I see no one's face but yours, and though you've been most loyal, it does get rather boring. Lucy, too, you'll come to visit, won't you? I rather like the notion. Everyone else is gone, y'know, and I've missed having family about. You'll spend the night, Lucy? Stay a day or two, perhaps, and tell me more about yourself. I should like that."

"Of course, your grace." Lucy didn't know whether to laugh or cry, and she reached out to take the elderly lady's hand in hers. Lucy recognized that despite her daily visits through the countryside and the omnipresence of Miss Somerville-Large, the Dowager Duchess of Mitford was a lonely lady, and Lucy knew that even if there was no family connection, she was going to get to know this lady well. "I should love to visit, your grace. Any time you like."

"Excellent. Now that that's settled, I must rest. Very tiring all this chatter, but don't worry, I shan't forget the letter, nor your visit. I never forget the important things." She rested her head against the nest of pillows and closed her eyes.

Lucy's hopes soared. She glanced toward the viscount and smiled; it was a positively wicked grin of triumph. Maybe, she thought, suppressing an equally wicked giggle, she wouldn't make a very good wife after all. She didn't know what had gotten into her, but she hadn't been in the least bit obedient of Dalsany's wishes this afternoon, and furthermore, she was quite glad for it.

The week concluded with a picnic on the hillside overlooking the Fleet, and after lunching on a cold collation beneath a blue-and-white-striped tent, the guests gathered at the shore of the sea loch as a troop of gillies appeared with an assortment of fishing creels and rods.

Mr. Pratt, whose greatest conceit was the silver cup he'd won two years before for the twelve-pound trout he'd caught while at a house party in Wales, was the first to clamor into a boat. To his dismay, young Miss Eglantine hopped in behind him, and before he might suggest that the girl remain ashore, for her incessant recitation of romantic poetry was bound to frighten away any fish, the little craft was gliding toward the center of the sea loch.

"Do sit down," Mr. Pratt instructed. "And try to be quiet."

"Yes, sir," Eglantine replied with a furious blush, altogether willing to do whatever he asked of her, even if it required baiting a hook in his behalf.

Back on shore, the viscount stepped into the second boat, and when he reached out to help Lucy, it was Lady Priscilla Fox Strangways, bedizened in an elaborate gown of pale purple muslin with an Amaranthus-colored parasol tucked beneath one arm, who took hold of his hand to gingerly board the boat. Where was Lucy? She was the one who'd organized this outing. Dalsany glanced up the hill and, satisfied to see her in the tent with his uncle, he turned back to Lady Priscilla. In point of fact, he rather liked the notion of having Lady Priscilla, who shared his dislike for fishing, in his boat instead of Lucy, who owned the most unladylike fondness for the pastime. He'd much rather float about and do nothing more than enjoy the quiet of the afternoon, and he was sure Lady Priscilla would consider time spent in such a fashion most worthwhile.

"Lady Priscilla, take care there, do move slowly." He helped her sit down upon the wicker seat in the center of the vessel.

"I do hope you don't mind that it's me," she crooned, and batted her eyelashes in such a manner that he knew it was going to be a most pleasurable afternoon, indeed. A roguish grin upon his face, the viscount pushed the boat away from the shore and began to row toward a thicket of rushes.

Several of the other guests were assisted into the remaining boats. A few of the bolder gentlemen donned waders and were escorted by a gillie into the nearby reeds to cast a line. Edith, having grabbed several slices of beef, fresh muffins, and two peaches from the remains of the picnic, set off for a walk toward the house. Only the earl and Lucy remained in the picnic tent.

His gaze rested upon her. She was the personification of a classic English afternoon, wearing a white corded muslin gown striped with yellow, her cheeks highlighted with delicate pink; and the silk ivy leaves entwined about the brim of a stylish straw bonnet matched her emerald-green eyes. How easy it was for him to see her sitting in one of those boats, fingers trailing in the water and reaching out to pick wild roses growing from the rocky outcrops along the shore. "How about it? There's one boat left. Care for a go 'round the Fleet?"

"I rather like it right here," she said as she sat back upon a wicker longue. Truth to tell, she'd seen the earl leaning more heavily upon his cane than the day before, and knowing how cramped those little rowboats could be, she thought it a far better idea to stay where they were.

Her response surprised him; he knew how well she used to love to fish. In an involuntary movement, his head cocked to one side as if to question the veracity of her statement.

Lucy knew precisely what the earl was thinking. "Well, yes, I do still like fishing, but I have to confess I'm a bit fagged. London seemed a constant go-round, but I didn't imagine country life could be nearly so hectic. I see there are several books in the hamper and would be perfectly content to read." She reached in and pulled out the first volume she touched. "I wouldn't mind if you went off. You're under no obligation to stay with me."

"Believe a bit of a laze sounds just fine." He took the book from her. Their fingers touched, ever so lightly, and experiencing a schoolboy rush of expectation, he looked down at the book. It was a copy of Shakespeare's *Sonnets*. "Do you have a favorite verse? I don't believe I've read these since my classics master required it in third form."

"The thirtieth," she replied. She, too, was aware of the sensation of his fingers brushing against hers. The contact was over as quickly as it happened, yet her fingers seemed to burn where his had touched them.

Opening to the thirtieth verse, he began to read aloud: "When to the sessions of sweet silent thought I summon up remembrance of things past." Unfamiliar with the verse, he was caught off guard, and when he reached the final lines his voice grew hoarse. "But if the while I think on thee, dear friend, all losses are restored and sorrows end."

Listening to the earl, Lucy experienced the sensation of every last ounce of air being robbed from her lungs. She had never heard those lines read with such tenderness of expression, and she knew the earl spoke from the heart as if he himself had penned those sentiments. The urge to touch him in some way, to let her hand rest upon his forearm or her fingers trail against his shoulder, was strong, but she didn't move. Instead she sat transfixed upon the paisley pillows and drank in the sight of him, the ink-black hair touched with silver, the strong jawbone and full masculine mouth, the deep sea-blue gaze and the piratical patch, and she thought she'd never seen anything quite so perfect before. A lock of silver-streaked hair fell across his forehead, brushing against that black patch, and at that moment, Lucy wanted nothing more than to take off that patch and look as deeply as she might into both his eyes. Her hand rose, then fell back to her side.

Aware of her intense scrutiny, the earl knew an uncharacteristic awkwardness. The book of sonnets dropped into his lap and, unable to meet her gaze, he focused upon the Fleet. There in the distance was a single boat, nearly hidden in a thick growth of reeds, and in the middle of the boat there was a bright purple parasol opened and situated in such a fashion that the craft's occupants were hidden. It didn't require a genius to know who was in that boat and what was going on. With a sideways glance the earl saw that Lucy was staring at the half-hidden boat, awareness etched upon her pretty face.

"Are you dreadfully jealous?" he asked softly, intending to offer solace but regretting the question right away. Better to have remained quiet, for he had no wish to upset Lucy any more than she must already be.

To his astonishment, a smile turned up the edges of her mouth and a funny little twinkle lit her eyes, for the most astonishing thing had occurred to her. In that moment, her confusion since arriving at Clovelly was explained, and she answered truthfully, "No, not at all."

"What?" He was flabbergasted.

"You must think me fickle and faithless and wholly without redemption but—" She couldn't finish. What was she to say? That she'd just discovered she didn't love Dalsany because she loved him? She turned scarlet and fumbled for an explanation, "I—I—"

"Don't worry, Minx, you're neither fickle nor faithless. Not in the least," he said, scarcely aware of what he was saying. "Not in the least." It didn't occur to him that Lucy might care for him. All he could think was that she couldn't love the viscount after all, not if she wasn't pea green with jealousy, not if she hadn't flown into the boughs over his reprehensible conduct. All he could think was that he could now act with a clear conscience to stop the wedding.

Eleven
❧❧❧❧

I T RAINED FOR TWO DAYS following the picnic, a much needed shower soaking the countryside, and when the dark clouds finally disappeared over the horizon the three girls went out in the pony cart. They would rather have gone down to the beach to see what the storm had brought ashore, but the earl forbade them to walk the cliffs. Cliff falls were never so bad as after a heavy rainfall.

"You're being an awful good sport about this, Lucy," pronounced Eglantine as they bounced through a puddle that rivaled the Channel in depth and another blanket of mud splashed their dresses.

"It's nothing a good washing can't take care of. Besides, weren't you simply going berserk being confined to the house?" Thank heavens, the earl had gone off on an overnight errand to Weymouth, or else she would have truly gone crazy shut inside Clovelly with him and trying to deal with the realization that she loved him and not her fiancé. As it was, guilt compounded by the prospect of marriage to a man she didn't love had been quite enough mental torment; the earl's presence in the house would have been unbearable. "Anything is better than another day inside."

Edith nodded and thought of Captain Pomeroy. He was quite fully recovered and eager to identify the double agent so that he might be done with his time in Dorset and return home to Buckinghamshire. The girl's feelings for the young captain had made her worldly in the ways of love, and now she wondered why Lucy had ever agreed to marry her brother. "No, silly, Eglantine wasn't talking about the poor roads. She means the codicil. You're being rather mild-mannered about Anthony and the codicil. I'd be livid, if I were you."

Lucy searched her brain to make sense of this conversation, but she couldn't recall anything about any codicil. The twins chattered as if she knew of what they talked. They volleyed their dialogue like a pair of tennis players.

" 'Course when Uncle Alex told us it suddenly made sense," Eglantine supplied.

"Truth to tell, we never did understand why Anthony was suddenly so eager to marry. It was quite a shock, y'know. Not that you aren't a gem, Lucy."

"Of course. A diamond of the first degree."

They shook their heads in accord, straw gold poke bonnets nodding in unison.

"But the notion of Anthony legshackled is rather incredible," said Edith.

"Wait. I'm not following any of this. What are the pair of you talking about? What codicil?"

The twins exchanged knowing glances. Eglantine, who was handling the ribbons, slowed the pony, and they both turned back to Lucy, who was riding in the rear seat.

"Uncle Alex's, of course."

"The one in his will, y'know, that says if Anthony doesn't marry and produce a child in such and such time he'll be disinherited."

"Your uncle stipulated that?" was Lucy's slow meditative query. "Marriage and a child were requirements, if Dalsany wished to be heir?"

" 'Course. How else was Uncle Alex to get Anthony to toe the straight and narrow?"

Giddiness washed over Lucy. Her thoughts were racing, and she was rather light-headed as she began to comprehend what they were saying. The most fantastic notion was taking shape in Lucy's brain. She almost giggled and raised a gloved hand to cover her mouth. "When was this codicil added?" she asked, but—if her hunch was correct— she already had a fairly good idea what the answer would be.

"Just a month or so ago, wasn't it, Edith?"

"Umm-huh," the redhead mumbled. "Just a month or so ago. Uncle Alex had his solicitor visit Anthony in Town and Mr. Frith explained the whole of it to him."

"And then your brother miraculously produced me?" was Lucy's conclusion as the pieces fell into place. Hers was to be a *marriage de convenance*. The viscount's proposal had been predicated on personal need, not love or affection or a shared vision of marriage and family. She was nothing more than a convenience to him, and a fortuitous one at that, to have so trustingly revealed herself to him. Lucy should have been outraged at this discovery, but she wasn't. The truth was the news of the codicil came as a profound relief, lifting the dreadful heaviness which she experienced whenever she considered the viscount and their future as man and wife.

"Precisely. He made quick work of it, and we were all mightily impressed."

"And you can imagine how shocked Uncle Alex was, especially with you being as nice as you are and not some strumpet hired to act the part."

"Pray, Lucy, you're not going to cry, are you?" cried Eglantine in tender alarm.

She shook her head in denial. Indeed, there were tears in her eyes, but it wasn't sorrow that filled her, rather an unbridled joy, for at last she was able to see her immediate future with a theretofore unknown clarity. The viscount didn't love her any more than she loved him; he merely needed a wife, any wife, to comply with this codicil, and as for herself, if anything, she had been in love with the notion of matrimony and having a family. That she had made a grave mistake, jumping far too quickly at the first offer of marriage, had become apparent since her arrival at Clovelly, but until this moment she had believed it was a mistake with which she would have to live forever. Her eyes lit with coming laughter. Now Lucy knew otherwise, and she began to laugh, tears of delight rolling down her cheeks, for this intelligence about the codicil was the very thing she needed to break off her engagement to Dalsany.

"I say, Lucy, it wouldn't be all that bad. You'd have a glorious title and oodles of blunt, and you do like my family and Clovelly. What more could you want?" The viscount had been trying, without success, to patch things up with Lucy for more than forty minutes. It was, however, looking rather grim, for there didn't appear to be any way to change her mind.

"But don't you see?" asked Lucy, trying for

the umpteenth time to make the viscount understand her decision to break the betrothal. Unable to speak of her unrequited love for another man, she focused upon her disdain for the bloodless arrangement he had been willing to undertake. "I want more out of marriage than that. More than you're willing to give."

He was perplexed, and his retort was rather petulant: "Can't imagine what." Then it occurred to him that she must be talking about love, and taking her hand in his, he essayed his most promising tone. "We could fall in love. That does happen, y'know."

"We *could*. And in the meantime, what would I have?" She tugged her hand free from his. Her studied and rational tone was reminiscent of a governess handling a young and prodigiously obstinate charge. "Or even worse, what if that never happened?"

"But I was sure you were wild for me, Lucy. You said so yourself, that I swept you off your feet."

"Yes, you did, but it wasn't love. You're handsome and funny, and you listened to my woes and took me seriously, but it wasn't love. Upon consideration, I fear I was in love with the notion of love," she said, sounding far older and wiser than she had that evening in the garden at Exeter House. She looked at him with genuine sympathy. Superficially, there were countless similarities between Dalsany and the earl, and in hindsight, it was easy for Lucy to understand why she had been so taken with the viscount. He was very much the image of the gentleman who had rescued her from the beach, very much the image of a younger Earl of Harrow, the image of the man with whom she had fallen in love—nay, perhaps, had loved these past years. "I'm sorry to be mucking up your plans, Anthony. Is your uncle going to make matters frightfully difficult for you?"

Momentarily, the viscount considered throwing himself upon Lucy's merciful and tender heart. If she knew the extent of his financial troubles, surely she wouldn't allow him to suffer the fate that awaited him if he failed to comply with the codicil. On the other hand, his vanity rather loathed the thought of painting himself in such an unfortunate light. At least, Lucy hadn't pealed a lecture over his head and gone off into some hideous display of righteous female indignation. She'd been rather reasonable, even if she had broken off their betrothal. He gave a shrug and forced a smile. "I'll bounce back."

"There's always Lady Priscilla," Lucy said in gentle reminder.

The viscount's visage brightened. Of course, why hadn't he thought of that? There was still time and enough to comply with the codicil if he set about courting Lady Priscilla straightaway.

"Why don't you pay her a call?" suggested Lucy. "I'm sure she'll be thrilled to hear the news of our broken betrothal."

"I believe I shall." He was grinning quite broadly, but possessed the modicum of tact necessary to suppress his pleasure just long enough to inquire, "But what about you, Lucy? What shall you do?"

"I, too, shall bounce back," she said in a fortified tone of voice, but inside she wasn't so certain. It was one thing to disentangle oneself from a disastrous betrothal, but quite another to produce an instantaneous alternative. It wasn't bad enough to fear that her love for the earl would never be returned. The truth was she didn't trust that emotion any more than she did her affection for Dalsany. What she'd mistaken for love with the viscount had been nothing more than enchantment with the notion of matrimony. Perhaps her sentiments for the earl were nothing more than a romantic attachment to the past. How disheartening that she was no more certain of her own feelings than she was of the earl's.

The glow she'd felt upon knowing she might break the engagement was fading fast, and she was having difficulty with a new host of unsettling emotions. She was beginning to feel cast adrift. Although she had passed her childhood without a home, she had, at least, had a place to call her own. The cottage in the cherry orchard had been an emotional anchor, it had always been there for her, and while living in its security, it had been safe to dream of a family and future beyond the orchard. But that was in her past and what she had come to rely upon of late was not hers to claim. She quite adored the Paget family and Clovelly, but she no longer had any right to be among them. Soon her visit would have to come to an end, and where would she go? What in heaven's name would she do with herself? Verily, it scarcely seemed possible, nay safe, to dare to dream anymore.

It was past eleven o'clock. The footmen had made their evening rounds to damp the fires and pull the draperies against the night air, and the household was asleep. Fast asleep, except for the earl, who had spent the evening sequestered in his private study, and his mother, who wished a word with her son. Finding the door to his study unlocked, Lady Bronwen did not scruple to knock. She entered unannounced.

The earl was seated behind his desk, a massive carved oak table in the Jacobean style. His good leg was firmly planted on the floor, the other one was elevated and extended, resting across the top of the massive piece of furniture. No lamps or candles were lit, and the only source of light in the room was the fire, which flared and sputtered at odd intervals to cast eerie shadows across the brooding expression upon the earl's face. He was a portrait of piratical splendor, all black and immovable, the only white being his shirt, opened at the neck.

"You're in pain?" Lady Bronwen asked from the threshold.

"Nothing out of the ordinary," he replied without turning to face her. He began shuffling more paper about the desk as if to imply there was some practical reason for being cloistered in his study at this late hour.

"Then it was cowardice that kept you away from dinner?"

He leaned forward in the chair and swiveled his upper body toward his mother, his gaze narrowed and his eyebrows shot toward the ceiling.

"Enow, Alex, don't feign incredulity, nor lack of comprehension." That Highland brogue was back once again. She closed the door behind her and went to stand before the desk. "It doesn't become you, Alex."

"Did you come to berate me?" he drawled in a voice that hinted of emotional exhaustion. He wouldn't call it cowardice precisely, but yes, he'd been avoiding the family, in particular Dalsany, for he didn't wish to become embroiled in a confrontation with the younger man. And he'd been avoiding Lucy as well, although his reasons for that were not so clear.

"Berate you? After a fashion, I suppose." Unruffled by the darkening glower upon her son's countenance, Lady Bronwen took a seat and continued. "I came to suggest that it would be appropriate for you to consider the consequences of your action and to ponder your responsibility in all of this."

"Ah." He raised a crystal brandy snifter, offered a salute, and drained the glass. He knew without asking that she was talking about the manner in which he'd allowed Lucy to hear of the details of the codicil from the twins and the subsequent broken betrothal.

Lady Bronwen wasn't deterred. "I assume you acted under the assumption that you were doing the right thing. It was planned, I suppose, for you had to have known that one word to either of the girls and Lucy would know the whole story in a trice."

"Is that a question or just a way to get 'round to voicing your opinion?" While this query was sharp, the earl, in truth, found it impossible to be truly angry with his mother. She was, after all, correct. He had put into motion a chain of events that would change their lives forever, and he had to accept that responsibility, although what it entailed remained a mystery.

"A bit of both." Her slender fingers toyed with the pearls at her neck. "It wasn't playing fair with Anthony, y'know. The lad did what you required of him and he thought his future secured."

"Don't worry, Mother, I won't throw him to the wolves. I'll see to his debts and set aside a new monthly stipend. He'll survive. He always does."

"And what about you?" The earl ignored this pointed query, and his mother expanded. "You're fully grown, no longer a child, yet your conduct concerns me, Alex. Not because I wish to censure, but because I care about you, as I care about every member of our family."

He appeared to take offense. "Are you suggesting my actions indicate I don't care about the family?"

"No. Only that perhaps for the first time in a very long while you allowed yourself to feel and to put those feelings before others. That's not a crime, you know, nor anything to be ashamed of."

The truth discomposed the earl, and as he stared into the fire he threaded shaky hands through his hair. "Tell me, Mother, am I this transparent to everyone?" His voice seemed to come from far away.

"No." She offered a tender smile. "Just to your mother."

He appeared relieved and settled against the back of the chair. A log on the fire hissed, popped, and then split, sending a trail of fiery red sparks onto the flagstone hearth; like a comet's tail across the sky the sparks instantly faded to black, but neither the earl nor Lady Bronwen noticed.

The lady broke the silence. "Of course, the more important question in all of this is what will happen to Lucy. Poor child. Her future, although you did not deem it bright, was at least secured as Anthony's wife and the future Countess of Harrow. Now what does she have? You may have liberated her from a loveless match and years of rustication without an attentive spouse, but what have you to offer her in return? Tell me—and do not answer too quickly." She raised a cautionary finger. "Tell me, do you love her?"

"I don't know." He sounded confused and tired, then a touch of hope laced his words. "I do care for her. Mightily. She was important to me once before, and of late she's become important again." The lines upon his face relaxed as he looked away from the fire, his voice brightened with a sense of awe. "I feel alive with her, Mother, willing to face the future."

"Willing to stop this nonsense about making Anthony your heir? Willing to do your duty and marry as you should and have a family of your own?"

"Are you suggesting that I propose to Lucy?"

Lady Bronwen's eyes twinkled. She gave a nod. "Something like that."

"Egad, Mother, I'm almost old enough to be her father and hardly the sort of figure of a gentleman a young lady like Lucy would wish to wed. She deserves a whole man."

The dowager countess made an exasperated noise. Sweet Lord, she had never realized her son could be such a monumental fool. "When did you acquire this propensity to overstatement, Alex? Enow, you're sounding worse than some tawpie. Old enough to be her father, you say. Fustian! An elder brother, perhaps. And as for your corporeal worthiness, that is something only Lucy should decide, and you must at least give her the chance. A little honesty wouldn't hurt either."

"Well, I suppose it's only fair to offer to help in some way," he said, feeling more confident than he sounded. His mother was right, although he wasn't about to give her that satisfaction. At least, not so soon.

"Only fair." Lady Bronwen tossed her hands

and shook her head in disbelief that any one gentleman, normally in possession of great intelligence, could be so simpleminded. For the time being she had done all that she could to bring the truth to light. Mayhap what was needed now was a bit of time. She stood to leave. ''Well, I suppose I should be grateful for that much. Good night, Alex, and good luck with whatever you decide regarding Miss Wickham.''

Twelve

❦ ❦ ❦ ❦

THE EARL OF HARROW'S SKILLS IN SEDUCTION had at one time been the tattle of Mayfair. Verily, his youthful affair with Lady Anne had appeared in all the betting books, for no other gentleman had satisfied the lady for more than a single night. After Lady Anne, there had been the Countess of Salisbury, several actresses, a ballet dancer, and the wife of the Swedish envoy. But as for more refined arts, he didn't own much experience. Hence his decision to talk to Lucy about her future was most unsettling, for he possessed not the vaguest notion of how to proceed. A summons to his study was far too impersonal—rather ominous, in fact—but an invitation to stroll along the cliff might be misconstrued as a romantic overture. A chance encounter, he decided, would be the best course, and so he set about doing everything possible to cross her path in an apparently unpremeditated fashion.

He didn't have to wait long. Shortly after dusk the next day, he went for his exercise in the plunge pool, and there he found Lucy seated on a marble bench at the edge of the pool, her straw bonnet, stockings, and Grecian sandals resting on the flagstone beside her. She was drying her feet.

The tap of the cane announced his arrival, and Lucy turned when he entered beneath the arched doorway. Their gazes met, and as always the sight of her disturbed him. Sweet heaven, how pretty she was, he thought, with those great green eyes widening in surprise, the pink upon her cheeks deepening, and her mouth parting as if to speak. But she remained silent. The fading light from the west shone behind her, lending an ethereal quality to her beauty, enhancing both her innocence and her desirability. The earl swallowed hard.

She had never looked more vulnerable than she did at that moment. The jonquil-yellow frock rucked up about her knees reminded him of another time, and he heard her voice from long ago: *I don't care for other people's opinions anyway.* The little girl had been the most fragile and lonely creature he'd ever known, but now he knew otherwise. This, not the long-ago moment, was her most vulnerable time, and *this was his doing.* Right or wrong, whether for good or bad reasons, he was to blame, and he didn't require his mother to remind him that he must accept that responsibility and do what was necessary to secure Lucy's future.

"Do you mind if I join you?" he asked, wondering if that pinched expression upon her face was a way of saying that she didn't care one jot what anyone said about her and Dalsany.

"No, please do," she replied. There was an odd little quiver in her voice she couldn't control. From where she sat he seemed as tall as the sky, towering over the world, dark and strong, ever her gallant pirate king, and there was something about the sight of him that fairly broke her heart.

The earl went to the bench. Tap tap. Lucy watched and there were tears in her eyes. This was the first she'd seen of him since she'd broken the engagement, and with this moment came the harshest reality of all. Not only was she going to have to leave Clovelly, but she was going to leave him, and that—she found her heart crying—was going to be unbearable.

"Pleasant evening, isn't it?" He rested his cane against the bench and sat down rather stiffly. He was feeling quite like the village idiot, hardly knowing what it was one said upon the occasion of a broken betrothal. His mother had wished him good luck with whatever he decided regarding Lucy, but the truth was he hadn't been able to decide anything. "Well, um, yes. I did hear about your news."

Silence descended between them, and Lucy stared as he threaded a hand through his hair. Why had he done it? she wondered. Why had he told the twins about the codicil? This question had been haunting her, and before she left Clovelly she needed to know why. She inhaled, counted to three, and allowed the question to pop forth from her mouth.

"Why did you do it? I didn't sleep a wink last night, you know, wondering about it. I kept asking myself that over and over again."

"Excuse me?" He nearly toppled off the bench. She couldn't be talking about the codicil, could she?

"Why did you tell Edith and Eglantine? I know it was you who told them, they said as much, and I'm not angry. It's really rather for the best. It's just that I was wondering why you said anything. Why you bothered." This query was magnified as it floated across the water.

The earl fumbled for a reply, and when he spoke his voice was unusually formal. "Because it was wrong to impose such a condition on Dalsany in the first place. Wrong because it wasn't fair to the girl he'd marry, and when it was you I—I—'' Egad, how did he say this? ''Well, I know the sort of young man Anthony's become, and it just seemed to me he wasn't the right fellow for you.''

''I see.'' His answer both confused and encouraged Lucy, and although they sat at opposite ends of the bench, the way she was reacting they might as well have been two inches apart. Her heart quickened, sudden color warmed her cheeks, and she leaned down to dip her hand in the pool, then she touched her face to cool off.

''Why not stay?'' he said without preface.

''At Clovelly?''

''Yes.''

''Is this a proposition?'' A funny smile tickled her mouth as Lucy realized the fantasy of being a pirate's wife was still vastly appealing.

''Of course it is.'' Then he proposed. Just like that. ''You see, Lucy. . . .'' He inched close enough to take her hand in his. ''I was hoping . . . Well, now that your plans to marry Anthony have been cancelled would you do me the honor and consider marrying me instead?''

Marry him? Marry Pip? Startled, Lucy gazed up at the earl, her eyes widened with amazement. She wasn't sure what she had expected him to say, but it hadn't been this, and she searched his face for some clue to his motivations. Wordlessly, they looked at each other. High above in the frescoed dome of the bathing grotto a pair of doves cooed, outside ewes bleated for their mothers and a dog barked, but Lucy didn't hear any of this. Her heartbeat was pounding in her ears, and she was capable neither of movement nor of speech as some invisible pulse charged the space between herself and the earl.

Her mind flew back to that Sunday on the roundabout. This moment was similar, and yet it wasn't, and Lucy wondered if the earl had ever wanted to kiss her. The thought left her breathless, and her mouth parted ever so slightly and her tongue darted out to moisten her lips. What was he thinking?

Desire for Lucy flickered through the earl, and he moved slightly to take her into his arms. For one brief moment, he heard an echo of the past— *I believe I'd like to marry you, sir*—then he focused upon the desirable young lady within his embrace, and lowering his head, he covered her moist mouth with his own. His lips were warm and firm as they moved over hers, one hand held her face and his fingers caressed her jaw as she began to tremble in his embrace.

Lucy moaned his name. "Alex," she called him on a soft breath, reaching up to entwine her fingers in his thick black hair. Things were happening to Lucy that had never happened before, and a strange hunger coursed through her.

The earl raised his head and gazed into her green eyes. That she was lovely to touch and taste and kiss was beyond his wildest dreams, but that she possessed such a sensual spirit was unexpected.

Lucy looked up at him with dreamy eyes, a little shy, a little concerned. His complexion was unusually pale and there were lines of strain about his mouth that she hadn't seen before. She waited for the earl to speak, to say something reassuring, elegant, anything with the tiniest element of romantic grace.

"I mean it does make sense," he said at last.

"Marriage, I mean. We're old friends and we get along well together. There's no sense in your leaving Clovelly."

Lucy's heart sank. It was sensible, yes, but nothing more, and when he didn't speak of love, when he didn't utter another word, she knew there was only one reply she could offer.

"Your proposal is a very kind gesture, but I must say no."

He was stunned by her rejection, and his arms fell away from her.

"And for the same reason that I broke off with Dalsany. You see, if I marry, it must be for love. Your offer is most generous and honorable, and I do appreciate your kindness, but I must decline."

As for her own emotions, could she trust them? Probably not. She hadn't loved Dalsany, but his proposal had blinded her to that, and it was unlikely that she had matured enough in the past few weeks to avoid that same folly. It didn't matter though, for unrequited love was as bad as no love at all, mayhap even worse. Again, she looked across the plunge pool. The sun was dropping fast, it was nearly beneath the tree tops at the edge of the wood, and the light in the grotto was fading rapidly.

"What will you do?" The bleakness in the earl's voice was as raw as it was unforeseen, and there was something else that sounded like an undercurrent of pain.

"I've written to Headmistress, and I hope to start my own school. It is what I know best."

"And when do you leave?" He dreaded her reply.

"In three days."

Not only had Lucy refused his hand in marriage, but she was soon to be gone. With that knowledge, it seemed as if the light had gone out of his life. To lose Lucy would be unbearable, and the earl knew then that he loved Lucy and the woman she had become. Reality struck him like a blow. Why else did he feel alive when she was by his side? Why else did his heart pulse with response at her laughter? Why was she the first and only female he had desired since his injury? He wished to marry Lucy and spend the rest of his life with her as friend and lover, confidant and companion.

"Three days! So soon?" he blurted out, knowing this love was real and his heart would break when she was gone. He grasped at any reason to keep her at Clovelly. "But what of your interest in finding out about your mother? What if the dowager duchess manages to contact Lady Thornton and she agrees to sail over from the Isle of Wight?"

"If something comes of her grace's correspondence, I can always return. In the meantime, I must get on with my life," she explained, knowing that it was not going to be easy to leave Clovelly. The longer she remained the more painful the eventual separation would be. She had to leave as soon as possible. "I shall return to the academy to make my plans, and if my own school does not become a reality, I'm sure Headmistress will have a position for me."

The resolve in Lucy's voice was the earl's final disillusionment, and he regarded her with infinite sadness. She had made up her mind, and to resort to further honesty and speak of his newfound love would be fruitless. They were not suited, and it was more than a matter of their age difference or his physical condition. He almost smiled at the irony of it, for those things that he had once imagined to be insurmountable barriers were not impediments after all. It was a matter of love, something he'd failed to reckon with altogether, and unless Lucy loved him—an outcome he had no inkling of how to effect under present circumstances—there was no hope.

Thirteen
❧ ❧ ❧ ❧

"SO, MY DEAR LUCY, it's stellar news. You've called off your betrothal to Dalsany," the gray lady said. There was a smile upon her face and a remarkable display of energy in her tiny voice. Truth to tell, the Dowager Duchess of Mitford had not sounded quite so chipper in many years.

"Yes, your grace," Lucy replied with as much patience as she could muster. This wasn't something she wished to discuss. Not only did the uncertainty of her future fill Lucy with anxiety, for she didn't really want to leave Clovelly, but the bareness of the earl's proposal filled her with despair, and she clung to the hope that the dowager duchess might have some promising news, anything to take her mind off the disaster she'd made of life.

Lucy and Lady Bronwen had accepted an invitation to luncheon at Aylesbury. The dowager duchess, being in receipt of a response to her missive to Lady Thornton, wished to share its contents with Lucy. They had, however, been seated in the conservatory for nearly thirty minutes, watercress soup and poached salmon had been served, and all her grace had thus far discussed was Lucy's broken engagement. The dowager duchess was propped against her usual nest of pillows, her luncheon plate was resting upon a footed tea tray balanced across her lap; Lady Bronwen, Lucy, and Miss Somerville-Large were seated at a wrought iron table beneath a bower of flowering orange trees, beside a pool in which giant black-and-gold carp circled and a trickle of water flowed from a vase in the arms of a marble Aphrodite.

"You're a wise young lady," the dowager duchess continued between infinitesimal bites of fish. She hardly ate enough to nourish a sparrow. "Mind you, I didn't know about the codicil, but I never did trust the nephew. Always was a bit of a *mauvais sujet,* and it doesn't surprise me that he pulled the wool over your eyes. Now don't get your dander up, Bronwen," she counseled in an aside, before once again focusing upon Lucy in explanation. "Bronwen always did dote on the lad, but he's rather too amusing for my liking. Selfish, too. Not in the least bit like you, my dear child. You haven't a selfish bone in your body, now, have you?"

Lucy paused in the process of daubing mustard sauce on her salmon. She demurred, "I assure you, ma'am, I'm far from model. I was one of Headmistress's most memorable students, and for the least laudable of reasons. I, too, had a penchant for climbing the orchard wall and visiting the beach," she confessed.

Her grace grinned. There was a touch of color in her cheeks this afternoon. "Know how to swim, do you?"

"Yes, ma'am."

"Ah, then I can better understand your curiosity about Lillibet."

At last, the conversation was turning to the subject of Lillibet and Lady Thornton. Lucy's visage brightened considerably. "Truth to tell, your grace, I have my hopes there may be some connection."

"Miss Somerville-Large, the letter, please." The dowager duchess relinquished her plate for an envelope from which she pulled a letter. "Here it is. The reply from Lady Thornton, and how good it was to hear from my old friend. She's doing well, she writes, and weathers the island winters better than one might expect. But you don't wish to hear that, do you, my dear child? Perhaps you'd like to read the letter for yourself."

Eagerly, Lucy took the proffered missive and scanned the front and back pages, then read them a second time to make certain she hadn't misunderstood their contents. "It says she has already begun preparations to leave the isle," she told Lady Bronwen. "Oh, ma'am, you must listen to this: 'I had long ago abandoned any hope that I might find my dear daughter after she ran off with that American, but to think she had a child and that this young lady of whom you speak may be my granddaughter is a joy I can scarcely comprehend.' " Lucy's voice caught and she required a few moments to compose herself before asking Lady Bronwen, "Do you think it's possible? Oh, why does she call him 'that American'? Why couldn't she use his name? Do you think 'that American' might be my father and Lillibet my mother?"

"It does seem possible," Lady Bronwen said. "Let us hope her omission of his name is not owing to a lapse in memory. However, we can do nothing more at this time save to pray that Lady Thornton will be able to tell us one way or the other when she arrives. When will that be, your grace?''

"She'll be here within a fortnight," chirped the dowager duchess, who seemed to have divested herself of twenty years at the prospect of Lady Thornton's arrival. "You do intend to stay on at Clovelly, don't you, dear Lucy?"

"I—I'm not sure. I had thought to leave day after tomorrow," was her unenthusiastic reply. She didn't wish to leave, but her determination to do what she considered right was evident in the stern set of her features.

"That won't do at all," said the dowager duchess. "No, no, not at all."

"Precisely what I've been telling her," put in Lady Bronwen. "She's become one of the family. I could not bear to see Lucy leave us. In my opinion, all this talk of founding a school—noble and self-sufficient though it may be—is the outside of ridiculous. Enow, enow." An uncharacteristic note of desperation crept into Lady Bronwen's voice. Usually, she could claim some modicum of control over her life and the lives of those around her, but not in this case, and she didn't like to contemplate what would happen—or wouldn't happen—if Lucy departed Clovelly before her son realized the truth and admitted it to Lucy. She was eager for any excuse to keep Lucy in their midst for as long as possible. "Totally unnecessary to go. Lucy has no need to work for her livelihood, none whatsoever. I wish her to stay on at Clovelly, and there should be no further discussion."

"Indeed, Lady Bronwen, how right you are." The dowager duchess gave an approving nod. "I trust you shall do everything necessary to persuade this young lady to remain."

"I shall endeavor," she promised, and Lucy, sitting quietly to the side, knew that it was going to be extremely difficult to go against the wishes of these two ladies.

At the dowager duchess's insistence, Lady Bronwen and Lucy stayed another full hour. The elderly gray lady, who chattered without cease, did not appear to tire, in fact, her excitement over the forthcoming visit of her old friend and sister-in-law rather invigorated her. Lucy heard about the Aylesbury hunt ball and how her grace had five times, in the previous century, won the coveted hunt cup. Lady Bronwen talked about the year she had married the earl and how the dowager duchess had welcomed her to the neighborhood with a gala masked ball. The ladies agreed that it was high time to revive some of the merry goings-on that had once been a regular aspect of social life along the coast, and with that the dowager duchess announced that she would hostess a summer gala; no, Lady Bronwen countered, although it would not be a betrothal ball, she intended to go ahead with her gala. Why not two galas? the dowager duchess suggested, and of a sudden, the social calendar of coastal Dorset did not appear so pale when compared to that of fashionable Mayfair.

Although it was a most pleasurable luncheon, Lucy couldn't suppress a growing sadness that lingered upon her heart. It was disheartening to consider that this might be the last time she visited Aylesbury, the last time she was part of such a convivial gathering of friends, and of a sudden, it seemed as if she were observing her surroundings from a very great distance. Wishing to capture this pleasant moment upon her mind's eye,

Lucy looked from her grace to Lady Bronwen and then to Miss Somerville-Large.

Gazing upon the aging companion, Lucy knew a sharp and wholly unanticipated pang of pity which quickly turned to apprehension at the realization that she had much more in common with the dowager duchess's poor relation that with her grace or Lady Bronwen. It seemed to Lucy that somehow in the past few days she had lost whatever independence she may have once possessed, and her plan to start a school was in direct defiance of this foreboding. Lucy could not help fearing that like Miss Somerville-Large she would have no other choice save to pass the remainder of her days relying upon the kindness of others. It was a somber prospect, and Lucy decided that if her life were to be that way she must get as far away from the earl and Clovelly as was possible. She had to start her school as soon as possible.

Some time later it was Lady Bronwen who initiated their departure from Aylesbury. "This has been a most enjoyable afternoon, your grace, but you must pardon me. I seem to be rather tired. A bit of a headache. I fear we shall have to be on our way."

"Are you all right, ma'am?" Lucy's voice rose in concern, her own worries fading into the background.

" 'Tis nothing more than this change in the weather." Lady Bronwen opened a fan and waved it about her face in a cooling motion. "I've always loved the spring, but the onset of summer does not sit well with me."

"Quite, quite." The dowager duchess bid her guests a regretful farewell, offering these enigmatic words for Lucy: "I trust you shall not leave Clovelly, dearest Lucy. I've a premonition about you, y'know. Have had one from the first. You were brought to us for a purpose, my dear child, and so it is that your future lies here. You must not tempt fate. You cannot leave.''

By the time the Paget landau wheeled to a halt at the horseshoe staircase, Lady Bronwen had become gravely ill. Tiny beads of perspiration dotted her forehead, and her head ached with such splitting ferocity that she could barely talk. Lucy summoned two footmen to assist the lady to her apartment in the west wing; there, Lady Bronwen reclined upon her bed and requested in a weak whisper that the damask curtains be drawn against the sun. A maid brought a basin of fresh water, and Lucy soaked a compress to place upon Lady Bronwen's forehead. She repeated this process several times before the dowager countess drifted to sleep and Lucy allowed herself to relax upon a nearby chair.

In her hurry to care for the dowager countess, Lucy hadn't paused to take off her bonnet, and she did so now, setting the satin creation on the nearest table. Several strands of hair tumbled free, but Lucy didn't bother to pin them back into place, she merely sat and watched Lady Bronwen, saying a silent prayer that whatever ailed the lady soon would pass.

''What happened?'' The earl's voice preceded him into the room, and he came to stand beside the bed. Worry was evident in the lines upon his face. His voice was tense. ''She's all right, isn't she?''

''I think so—I don't know—'' Lucy replied, flustered by his unexpected presence. Although the earl had been on her mind since she'd rejected his proposal, she hadn't considered what might happen or what she might say when next they met. Unprepared for this encounter, she focused upon the immediate situation. "Everything seemed fine. Our visit with the dowager duchess was most pleasant, then your mother complained of a headache and it has only gotten worse. The pain, I fear, has become excruciating."

He moved nearer the bed, set aside the cane, and rested his weight against the mattress in order to lean closer to his mother. "Mother, are you awake?"

"Alex, is that you?" She was half asleep and did not open her eyes.

"Yes, Mother. I came as soon as I heard you weren't feeling up to snuff." He took her hand and gave it a squeeze, then placed a silver bell in her grasp and closed her fingers about it. "You're to get a good rest, and if you need anything, just give a ring."

In the morning, however, Lady Bronwen's condition had not improved, and a message was dispatched to Dr. Parke in Weymouth, who arrived posthaste to spend a full hour with the patient while the earl and Lucy waited anxiously in the west wing corridor.

"She is very weak," the doctor informed them in a grave tone when he had exited the room and shut the door behind him. "And you must do everything to keep her content and comfortable. No excitement, and nothing to upset her in any way."

"But what is it?" inquired the earl.

"I can't say for certain, but this bears a distinct similarity to a case I saw while I was in medical school."

"Well, out with it, man, what was it?" was the earl's impatient query.

"In that particular incident, it was a tumor upon the brain."

Lucy's stomach plummeted, and she raised both hands to cover her gaping mouth. Beside her, the earl groaned, and she glanced at him, noting the taut muscles along his jaw, his narrowed gaze, and the sudden leap of outrage upon his countenance.

"No," he declared, and his grip about the cane tightened as he gave the floor a ferocious thwack.

Lucy stepped back, her instinct to offer solace thwarted by the violence of his reaction. Instead, she stood, silent and watching, a pain growing within her at the thought of Lady Bronwen's physical agony and the mental anguish her loved ones would suffer if her disease was, indeed, that severe.

"Lady Bronwen has made a request, sir. She wishes to see Miss Wickham." Lucy nodded, and she and the earl moved toward the door, but the doctor stopped the earl. "Just Miss Wickham, sir. Alone. Your mother was very specific."

Lucy glanced up at the earl and whispered, "I won't be long." She entered the darkened room. It was unbearably stuffy, a single branch of candles burned on the mantel, and the nasty odor of sulfur clung to the air.

"Is that you, dear Lucy?"

"Yes, ma'am." She hurried to Lady Bronwen's bedside. "You wished to see me?"

"I've a favor to ask of you, dearest Lucy." The counterpane was tucked about her waist and, garbed in a silver nightgown, her hair unpinned and a single braid resting across one shoulder, she was a very different woman. The pearls she always wore were not there, revealing a thin and wrinkled neck, and she appeared much older and frailer than she had been only the day before. "Will you cancel your plans to leave? Will you stay at Clovelly? *You must say yes.* Alex isn't prepared for my death. He will need you."

"Oh, no, ma'am, you aren't going to die," was Lucy's quick retort. So concerned was she with refuting Lady Bronwen's reference to death that she hadn't even heard what the lady had said about her son. "You mustn't speak like this. It's not healthy. You shall follow the doctor's orders, all of them to the letter, and I'm sure you'll be up and about in no time. And you mustn't talk about dying. Not another word."

"Enow, who can predict?" Lady Bronwen replied in faint rejoinder. "Nothing in life is certain. Even a cough can be fatal."

Lucy didn't know what else to say. After all, Lady Bronwen was right. She took the older lady's hand in hers and listened as she spoke.

"You must do this one favor for me. And it's not just Alex I'm worried about. It's Edith and Eglantine, too, y'know. Those poor girls. They're still so very young and growing up without their parents has been difficult for them."

Lucy's reaction was odd. She busied herself plumping up the lady's pillows. "What can I do for you? Read to you, perhaps?" The idea of making another promise to anyone was disconcerting, and although she didn't wish to deny Lady Bronwen, she'd much rather avoid making any more promises. She fiddled with the pillows some more. "There, how is that?"

"You mustn't fuss over me," she scolded weakly. "It's the others who will need your care. You must promise to stay and watch over them."

In spite of herself, Lucy couldn't refuse. "Yes, ma'am, I promise."

"And you'll look after the twins and Alex for me?"

"I'll try." Such an undertaking might have been an unwanted burden to most young ladies, but it appealed to Lucy's maternal instinct. It was a natural call to duty, and although she knew the dowager countess needed to *hear* her promise more than anything else, Lucy still liked the notion that she was needed. More importantly, it allowed her to put off leaving Clovelly to face an uncertain future; it allowed her to remain a bit longer among those of whom she'd grown immeasurably fond. "Thank you, ma'am."

"Why ever would you thank me?"

"Because I didn't really want to leave," she confessed.

And Lady Bronwen closed her eyes, comforted in the knowledge that she was doing the right thing.

Dinner that evening was a bleak affair. Everyone was acutely aware of the empty chair at the head of the table, and conversation was spotty at best; even the servants were subdued as they entered and exited the dining room bearing silver platters of roast lamb and minted spring carrots. There was some small talk about the weather, but no one dared to bring up Lady Bronwen's health. It wasn't until dessert was served that the earl explained Dr. Parke's diagnosis: it would be a matter of weeks before anyone could definitively identify Lady Bronwen's malady, and regardless of the doctor's final conclusion, the earl stated he would never allow any sort of surgery to be performed on his mother. Eglantine began to cry, Edith gave a watery sniffle, and the viscount loudly protested that this was not the sort of discussion one wished to hear while dining.

"I suggest that if the current situation isn't to your liking, Anthony, you might wish to quit Clovelly," said the earl. "Mother needs our support, not—"

"Speaking of leaving," Lucy cut in. This seemed as good a time as any to inform everyone of her decision to stay. Besides, she didn't like it when the earl and the viscount squabbled. "Lady Bronwen spoke to me this morning, and she has asked that I change my plans, so I've written to Headmistress and told her that I shall remain at Clovelly for as long as Lady Bronwen wishes."

"That's most generous of you," said the earl; his composed voice did not reveal any trace of his inner excitement. Now he knew what it was that his mother had discussed with Lucy, and despite his genuine fears for his mother, a sense of well-being enveloped him. He hadn't wanted Lucy to leave, nor had he wished to pass the next few weeks alone, waiting to see if his mother recovered and being the one to put on a brave face for Edith and Eglantine.

"I've grown most fond of your mother, sir, and could not leave under the circumstances." Lucy's reply was as formal as his.

The twins, however, did nothing to mask their excitement at Lucy's news, and their jubilation put a happier edge on the evening. They rose from their seats to hug Lucy, and all three girls allowed their tears to flow freely. They cried with sorrow at the tragedy of Lady Bronwen's illness and they cried with relief at the knowledge that they had each other for comfort. As Lady Bronwen had intended, Lucy's announcement had managed to put a somewhat brighter face on a gloomy situation.

Only Dalsany wasn't pleased with the development, a fact that was evident in his harassed expression. He didn't relish the prospect of confronting one of his failures over kippers each morning, and Lucy was, indeed, his most grievous failure. A fact of which he did not wish to be reminded. Furthermore, Lady Priscilla Fox Strangways, with whom he'd made promising romantic progress this afternoon, had a virulent jealous streak, and he feared she might not understand why Lucy remained in residence at Clovelly, a situation which could jeopardize the proposal he intended to make before the week's end. Needing to consider his strategy vis-à-vis Lady Priscilla, Dalsany excused himself from the table without explanation. The twins, who had promised to pay a call upon Lady Bronwen, followed their brother out of the dining room, and the earl and Lucy were left alone.

Lucy set her damask serviette on the table. It was one thing to agree to stay, but it was quite another to spend time in the earl's company. It was far too painful, and she hurried to leave, but the earl extended his arm as if to prevent her from rising.

"Please stay a few moments," he said. "There's something I wish to discuss with you."

Her heart skipped a beat and she gazed at him in hopeful expectation. How she longed for him to propose once again, and this time to declare his love. How she longed to hear him say that he cherished her above all other women and wished to marry her for naught but love. "Yes?" she asked, knowing such wishes were in vain, but being nonetheless unable to prevent herself from entertaining such fantasies.

"I've been considering your plans to start a school," he began in a stilted tone. This wasn't going to be as easy as he'd imagined when he made up his mind about what he intended to do regarding Lucy. After much consideration, he'd decided that the best way to show his true affection for Lucy would be through respect and support. It made sense. Men who didn't truly care for their wives gave little credence to their aspirations, nor did they encourage independence of action. He had come to realize that the greatest gift of love was allowing a loved one to be free. Lucy had made it abundantly clear that she wished to leave Clovelly and start a school, hence the earl had decided to support her in this endeavor.

"It is a courageous and admirable decision. You've always been a singular young lady, Lucy, and I know you shall succeed at whatever you do."

Lucy replied with a thin smile and watched as he leaned down to pick up something off the floor. It was a flat velvet box, and he set it on the table before her. She looked at him in some confusion. It was a jewelry box, and she couldn't imagine why he would be giving her a gift.

"Go on. Open it," he urged.

She complied, emitting a small gasp of wonder as she beheld a most astonishing ruby-and-diamond necklace. There were four large rubies, configured in a rose floral pattern, and each cluster was surrounded by diamond leaves. Candlelight glimmered off the precious stones, making the exquisite design of blood-red roses glisten as if touched by a morning dew. "I've never seen anything so lovely before. It's utterly unique."

"Quite," he replied in a low voice, silently adding that they were as unique as Lucy herself. "The Harrow Rubies, and I want you to have them."

"A family heirloom? But I couldn't take them. I've no right. Whatever would your mother say?"

"Mother knows. I told her I intended to give them to you and she heartily endorsed my decision. You must think of them as collateral, a nest egg of sorts to guarantee your future."

"But I could never sell them. It wouldn't be right."

"And you shan't have to. Merely owning the Harrow Rubies should satisfy any banker that you would be a good customer, and as I know your school shall succeed, I've no fear you'll sell the rubies. They'll be in good hands."

"I don't know what to say." While he hadn't declared his love, nor fallen on one knee to plead that she change her mind and agree to marry him, this gift affected her profoundly. It revealed a depth of admiration and trust that she considered as priceless as the rubies themselves, and for that, she found herself falling ever deeper in love. Tears welled in her eyes and she rose to go and stand before his chair.

"Thank you," she whispered. Then she leaned down and kissed him upon the cheek.

He smiled, secure in the knowledge that he had done the right thing. It was only a small step toward his final goal, but he sensed a new closeness with Lucy, and despite his mother's illness, he couldn't help feeling that the future was not as bleak as it had once seemed.

Fourteen
❧ ❧ ❧ ❧

IT WAS TRUE! Lucy wished to stand on the cliff and shout the news to all the world. Lady Lillibet was Lucy's mother, and Lady Thornton, a plump white-haired woman with deep green eyes and the gentlest smile Lucy had ever seen, was her grandmother. They had been reunited in Lady Bronwen's west wing apartment, the dowager duchess and Lady Thornton having agreed to meet with Lucy at Clovelly.

"It would give me great pleasure to be with you when you meet Lady Thornton," Lady Bronwen had said when they received news of the lady's arrival from the Isle of Wight. "And as I cannot endure the ride to Aylesbury, you must pen a reply without delay and invite them to join us here at Clovelly as soon as they are able."

Lucy had done as Lady Bronwen requested, and the Dowager Duchess of Mitford and her sister-in-law, Lady Thornton, came to tea the following day. Everything about their visit surpassed Lucy's wildest dreams, and for two glorious hours all the pain and regret owing to her unrequited love for the earl was forgotten as she learned about her parents and came to know her grandmother.

The locket was the final confirmation, Lady Thornton having at first been reluctant to accept the truth. "Yes, my dear," she told Lucy, "You look very much like my darling girl Lillibet. Quite nearly the exact image of her at your age. It was the year of her come-out, y'know. The year she eloped, and the last year I ever saw my darling girl. Yes, there is a strong resemblance, uncanny, but after so much time how can I be certain? It may be that I wish to believe, you see," she said, each word ringing with a lifetime of sorrow as a host of memories returned to the lady. On a melancholy sigh, she offered Lucy her singular smile. It was gentle and kind and bespoke a giving nature. "I do not mean to be cruel, but I would not wish either of us to be disappointed or deceived, and having heard of your broken betrothal, I would not wish to be the cause of any more pain."

Lucy sat primly, her back as straight as it would go, her hands demurely folded upon her lap. She knew Lady Thornton was right to be cautious, yet she could not suppress her self-doubt, nor the horrible feeling that she must have done something dreadfully wrong for which she was now paying. She even considered that it might be as that horrid Lady Mersham had said: she was such a nonentity that no one would want her, not even her very own grandmother.

"Lucy dear, show Lady Thornton the locket," Lady Bronwen urged from her bed. Although the dowager countess was still confined to her apartment and the doctor remained unable to offer a definitive diagnosis, she appeared better with each passing day, the particular news that her son had given Lucy the Harrow Rubies having produced an immediate improvement in her appetite and coloring.

"Have you ever seen this locket, ma'am?" Lucy pulled the gold locket from beneath the bodice of her muslin gown and over her head. For an instant, she stared at the locket, and in that moment, her childhood longing for mother and family was revealed, then she handed it to the white-haired lady sitting beside her on the ivory damask settee.

No one breathed, or moved, as Lady Thornton turned the locket over in the palm of her hand. "Oh, my dear, my dearest dear," she exclaimed in a tearful voice, clutching the locket to her breast with one hand as she pulled Lucy into her embrace with the other. "I should never forget this pretty trinket, not in a million years. Never. We had her initials engraved upon the backside. See, C.E.A. Caroline Elizabeth Alyce. Lillibet was an affectionate name. Her baby nurse called her that. She was such a little thing that we all thought the name quite perfect. Oh, my dear child, there can be no doubt now that you are mine. My own dearest granddaughter. This is a true miracle and a cause for celebration."

All the ladies cried a bit. Although it was neither ladylike nor good ton to display such emotion in public, this was, after all, an exceptional occasion. Besides which, who among them cared about such things? Lucy showed her grandmother the letter written by her mother before her death, and Lady Thornton, after another bout of tears, informed Lucy there was a small inheritance to which she was entitled. Her father, she learned, had, indeed, been an American. Charles Drinker Wickham was the son of a distinguished and wealthy Philadelphia family to whom Lady Thornton had written countless times in an effort to learn what had happened to her daughter. No one had ever replied, and after many years, she had come to suspect that her husband had never allowed a single one of those letters to be posted.

"It seemed as if Lillibet and Charles had vanished off the face of the earth. I could find no trace of them. We knew they were wed at Gretna Green and they sailed shortly thereafter on one of your father's ships, but to where I never discovered. The Wickhams had a prosperous business in the China trade, tea and spices and such, and your father had been in London on business when he met Lillibet at Lord and Lady Palmerston's annual rout. I did try to find them. Truly I did, but my husband and his brother forbade me from searching, you see, and there was very little a lady on her own could do without the benefit of a man."

"But why, ma'am? I don't understand. Why would anyone forbid you to find your own daughter?"

"Charles was an American," put in the dowager duchess as if that alone explained the whole of it. "My husband, the duke, was the eldest brother, and your grandfather, Lucy, was the youngest, but there was another son, Henry, who perished on board a warship in the Chesapeake Bay. The vessel was attacked and sunk by an American privateer during that dreadful war for independence, and neither my husband nor his brother ever forgot or forgave Henry's death. Every American remained their enemy."

"And when my dear Lillibet, sweet and innocent and carefree, committed the unpardonable sin of losing her heart to an American—indeed, to the most dashing male specimen in the West End that season—the duke demanded we put a stop to the relationship. It was callous, and, of course, Lillibet had always been a bit of a rambunctious thing, doing as she pleased without fear of disapproval. Charles was a perfect gentleman and I was certain he loved Lillibet and would make her happy." Lady Thornton began to cry again.

"Now, Charlotte, you must stop that," said the dowager duchess. "There's been quite enough crying for one afternoon, and I'll thank you for stopping. Never did like watering pots and I always did like you, so you must stop."

"Indeed, this is a time for rejoicing," said Lady Bronwen. "A time—as you, Lady Thornton, so aptly stated—for celebration." Then she shocked them into momentary speechlessness. "I do believe I shall proceed with my gala ball after all. Of course, it won't be in honor of Lucy and Anthony, rather in honor of Lucy and Lady Thornton, to celebrate their reunion."

"But, ma'am, are you sure? Your health. Do you think Dr. Parke will—"

"I don't care what the doctor thinks. The invitations have been sent, the musicians engaged, and much cooking has already been done. There's no sense in letting it all go to waste. Furthermore, it would give me much pleasure, and if the doctor wishes me to recover, I'm sure making me happy is part and parcel of any cure."

"All right, Bronwen, we shall agree to your ball, but only if you allow Charlotte and Miss Somerville-Large to oversee the details. You must not get overtired, for if the ball is to be at Clovelly you must act as hostess. You must at least be well enough to make an appearance on the musicians' gallery and wave to your guests."

"It would be exceedingly foolish of me to refuse such a gracious offer. So we are agreed, there shall be a gala ball at Clovelly in eight days' time?"

The ladies nodded in accord, and Lady Bronwen smiled in the certainty that matters were very close to concluding precisely the way she would have them.

"I shall miss you all when I am returned home," Captain Pomeroy said. It was the day before the ball, which the earl had decided would be the perfect opportunity for the captain to determine whether or not the double agent was in their midst, and Lucy and Edith had brought him a set of elegant evening clothes for the occasion.

"Will you return to visit?" asked Edith.

Lucy looked at the red-haired twin and noted how changed the girl was since she had arrived at Clovelly. Her voice was quieter, her walk more sedate, and she no longer wore her hair in pigtails, but combed it free and tied it back at the nape of her neck with a simple white satin ribbon. Edith had become a young lady, causing Lucy's heart to ache. Lucy knew it was Edith's affection for Captain Pomeroy that had brought about this change, and she prayed young Edith would not suffer in love as she was suffering. She studied the young man and queried, "Yes, Captain, will you return?" The expression upon his face banished any doubt that he did not hold Edith in equal affection, and Lucy, having never seen a gentleman blush, smiled.

"Yes, I should like to return to Clovelly. Although my stay has been one of confinement, I've enjoyed the company and what little I've seen of the environs is lovely. I should like to see more one day. Tell me, Miss Wickham, do you know if Lady Bronwen and the earl plan to take Lady Edith and her sister to London for their come-out next year?"

"I could not say, sir. Much would depend, I suppose, upon the dowager countess's health."

"Ah, yes, quite."

"Would you come to Town, Captain Pomeroy, if I were there?" Edith dared to ask.

"Verily, Lady Edith," he replied. "It would be an honor."

For a moment, Edith and Captain Pomeroy stared at one another as if no one else were in the room, then Lucy coughed ever so delicately, and they looked toward her. "The earl has asked me to remind you, Captain Pomeroy, that he shall introduce you as a distant cousin come to escort Lady Edith to her first ball. Mr. Pratt, the organist in Fleet Regis, shall escort Lady Eglantine."

A dark expression clouded the captain's countenance. Although he would like to escort Lady Edith, his duty came before pleasure, and he hadn't planned on socializing in such a visible manner. He'd expected to circulate through the crowd of his own accord, but he supposed the earl knew best. "This Mr. Pratt, is he your sister's beau?"

"Eglantine likes to think so. Although I often tease her and say the only reason he pays the slightest attention to her is so that he gets invitations to Clovelly."

"A bit of a parvenu?"

"The most dreadful mushroom, yes. And the most wretched busybody. Grandmother loathes him, and Eglantine is a wet goose to pay him any heed.''

The captain appeared to cogitate upon this piece of intelligence before turning to Lucy and commencing an entirely different line of discourse. 'I'm told, Miss Wickham, that you, too, shall soon be departing Clovelly,'' he said, being far too much of a gentleman to hint that he had any knowledge of her broken betrothal.

''Yes, I shall. The ball is as much a farewell as a celebration. I've decided to travel to the Isle of Wight with my grandmother, Lady Thornton, and there at Mottistone I shall found a school for young ladies. Lady Thornton's home is large enough for at least fifteen students, and my grandmother has been lonely for many years. It's an arrangement that suits us both.''

''But you will return to visit?'' This came from Edith. Although she'd been happy for Lucy when she found her grandmother, Edith was still selfish enough not to want to lose her new friend. ''Besides, you won't go right away, will you? What about our grandmother?''

''No, I shan't leave straightaway. Not until we know Lady Bronwen is all right. Although I must say, she appears to be doing quite splendidly, don't you agree?''

''Yes, and I think that horrible old doctor lied about a tumor.''

''Doctors are not infallible,'' injected Captain Pomeroy. ''Let us pray he was incorrect. I should like to meet your grandmother, Lady Edith, and get to know her, for everything you've told me about the lady makes her sound most admirable. I know I should like her.''

''Oh, indeed, sir, and Grandmother would like

you, but never so much as I," Edith declared in a burst of ingenuous adoration.

Lucy's heart contracted. "Excuse me," she mumbled, "I've just remembered something I must do." She hurried from the room before Captain Pomeroy or Edith saw the tears threatening to stream down her cheeks.

In the sanctuary of the dim corridor, she collapsed against a recessed doorway and surrendered to her anguish at the knowledge that such a tender and pure love would never be hers. Granted the earl had revealed his respect when he gave her the Harrow Rubies, but that wasn't enough for Lucy. She wanted it all. Even the joy of finding her grandmother and learning about her parents could not assuage her heartbreak. How ever, Lucy wondered in despair, was she to survive tomorrow's gala ball when she hardly felt like celebrating?

Fifteen

❧ ❧ ❧ ❧

L UCY WAS AS READY AS SHE'D EVER BE to go
downstairs and take her place in the receiving line in the marble rotunda. She stood for a
moment at her open window, looking not toward
the dark waters of the Channel but around the
corner toward the front of the house, where she
caught a glimpse of the drive clogged with vehicles and illuminated by great flaming torches. For
the past thirty minutes, she had been aware of
the grate of carriage wheels on gravel, an occa-
sional ripple of laughter, or the undercurrent of
voices mixing with the distant crash of waves. It
was a fine evening for the gala, clear skies and
fair, and Lady Thornton, who had arrived earlier
in the day, opined that everyone who had been
invited would be in attendance. Carriages had
arrived from as far afield as the Somerset border,
and every guest room—be it public or private—
within a twenty-mile radius would have an oc-
cupant this night.

"I've something for you, my dear child," announced Lady Thornton upon entering Lucy's
bedchamber. A manservant followed; he carried
an enormous box, which he set upon the bed, and
as the lady opened it she told Lucy, "I hope you

will be pleased and agree to wear this.'' She produced an exquisite ball gown in pearl Nakara silk with deep scarlet roses at the shoulders and about the hem. ''It was your mother's although it grieves me to say she never wore it. Lillibet and Charles eloped before the modiste delivered it. I never told anyone I kept it. It was silly of me, I know, and even sillier to have brought it with me from Mottistone. You see, I had hoped that you would, indeed, be Lillibet's child and that you would agree to wear her dress. It was silly, and while half of that wish has been granted, I dare not harbor hope—'' Her elderly voice broke off in uncertainty.

Lucy was infinitely touched. ''No, you're not silly at all, ma'am. Not in the slightest. And I should be honored to wear my mother's dress. Besides, it's quite the loveliest gown I've ever seen.''

The fit was perfect, and now as Lucy turned away from the window she went to stand before the pier glass one last time. The pearl-colored gossamer dress was draped over a silver satin slip and embellished with a train, opening up in front and tied with small bows of silver satin. The long sleeves were gathered into a puff at the shoulders and clasped with embroidered roses in rich scarlet and silver and ivory, and the bottom of the skirt and train were likewise ornamented with scarlet roses shot with silver threads. In her pale gold hair, swept into a cascade of loose ringlets and worn à la Venus, there were real scarlet roses entwined with hothouse gardenias. About her neck Lucy wore the Harrow Rubies. How could she resist wearing them when they matched so perfectly, and when she would probably have very few other opportunities to wear them?

"We're here!"

The twins descended upon Lucy's room.

"Oh, do look, Lucy. Aren't our dresses ever so grand?"

They were wearing similar high-waisted gowns of white satin. Eglantine's was accented in Clarence blue and there were gillyflowers in her midnight-black hair, while Edith's gown was edged in gold and clusters of stark white blossoms graced her lustrous red hair. They had taken much care with their toilette on this special occasion, and both were chattering like magpies.

"Do you think there will be a mention of Grandmother's gala in one of the London papers?" queried Eglantine.

"No doubt there shall be," replied Lucy.

Eglantine sighed. "And my name? And Mr. Pratt's, do you think?" There could be no finer addition to her scrapbook than a clipping in which her name was mentioned in the same paragraph with Mr. Pratt's.

"No, I don't think," retorted Edith. "We're not out, and you know very well that it wouldn't be proper to mention either of us. And as for your Mr. Pratt, you must realize, Eglantine, that he's of no consequence."

"You're just jealous because Uncle Alex had to dig up some distant relative to be your escort!"

To Eglantine's disappointment, this barb failed to produce its desired affect. Edith merely smiled, and so the dark-haired twin focused upon Lucy, the sight of the older girl causing her to momentarily forget herself.

"You look like a bride," Eglantine said in awe.

"Of course she looks like a bride," agreed Edith. "That's why she's wearing the rubies, isn't it?"

Lucy picked up her gloves and scolded, "The two of you are talking in riddles again. It's most impolite, y'know."

"Oh, Lucy!" gasped Eglantine. "Don't say Uncle Alex didn't tell you about the rubies!"

Butterflies took flight in Lucy's stomach. "Was there something he should have told me?" She phrased her question with care.

"The *legend* of the Harrow Rubies," Eglantine intoned, as dramatic as always.

"Good heavens, they're not haunted, are they?" Her hands darted upward to touch the ruby-and-diamond roses where they rested upon her creamy neck.

"No, they're not haunted. Not precisely. But Uncle Alex would be cursed if he broke the vow."

"If he didn't give the necklace to the woman he loved."

"It's only for love matches, you see. Though the rubies were designed more than a hundred years ago by one of our ancestors for his bride, they've only been worn by five countesses."

A tiny smile of wonderment graced Lucy's lips. *For love matches?* A special sparkle of hope reflected in her eyes. "And, tell me, does your uncle believe in such things?"

"Of course he does," the twins declared in one affirmative voice.

Lucy told herself their chatter was nothing more than adolescent nonsense. Both girls fancied themselves in love, and of late they viewed everything with an overly romantic eye. It was, nonetheless, a delightful prospect to consider that the earl had actually given her the Harrow Rubies because he loved her, But, she reasoned with caution, it would be foolhardy to put any stock in such a thing. Leaving Clovelly was going to be painful enough without compounding her unhappiness with false hope. Hence Lucy merely smiled at the twins, asked them if they were ready to join the festivities, and the three young ladies moved toward the marble rotunda.

"I should like to visit Lady Bronwen first," Lucy said when they reached the corridor to the musicians' gallery.

"Go ahead," Edith and Eglantine chimed, and eager to join their escorts, they proceeded downstairs.

Lucy passed through a low door and onto the musicians' gallery, a small balcony area overlooking the marble rotunda with a gilt railing and magenta velvet curtains drawn back. In the past it had been used for small quartets and could accommodate the usual number and assortment of musicians that comprised a string ensemble. The walls were painted in an elaborate fresco. Cherubs, some carrying harps or flutes, others holding lyres, lounged upon large pink-and-white clouds floating in a deep blue sky.

This evening, the musicians' gallery was reserved for Lady Bronwen, while the orchestra had been moved to a raised dais at the opposite side of the marble rotunda. In the gallery, several chairs were positioned for guests who wished to pay their respects to the dowager countess. Although a longue had been provided for Lady Bronwen's comfort, she was sitting upright on a chair when Lucy entered. The lady, wearing her signature triple strand of pearls, looked elegant and reassuringly healthy. A smile of deep warmth and affection lit her face at Lucy's arrival.

"How lovely you are, Lucy. Your grandmother must be most proud, and may I admit to my own touch of pride."

"Thank you." Lucy curtsied, then dropped a kiss on the lady's brow.

"And it pleases me mightily to see you wearing the Harrow Rubies."

Lucy had to ask, "Pray, ma'am, is it true about the rubies?"

She knew of what Lucy spoke and her smile deepened. "Of course, it is. Why ever did you imagine I was so pleased when Alex gave them to you? He loves you very much, y'know. Oh, you mustn't look so surprised. Mothers know these sorts of things. And while I long feared he might never understand it, when he decided to give you the rubies I knew he had at last realized the true direction of his sentiments."

"But why hasn't he said anything to me?" Lucy's heart was racing.

"Pride, no doubt, and a touch of fear, too, I suspect. Love can be most daunting, y'know."

Lucy nodded. She understood only too well.

"Pray, what do you plan to do about it, Lucy?"

"I—I'm not at all certain."

Lady Bronwen gave Lucy's hand a reassuring pat. "Just remember this need not be a farewell ball. Now hurry downstairs to join your grandmother and the others. You should not miss a moment of your celebration."

At midnight, the footmen opened the doors to the long gallery. Supper was announced, and as the guests helped themselves to such treats as glazed duckling and roasted beef, strawberry tarts and pyramids of marzipan cakes, they remarked upon the decor. The buffet table was decorated with a nautical motif, fleets of tiny sailing ships floated on mirror lakes down the center of the table amidst papier-mâché mermaids and whales, starfish and sea horses.

Lucy sat at a small circular table by the opened windows with her grandmother and two young lordlings, Burnham and Wyatt, who were doing their utmost to impress Lucy as she nibbled on a marzipan starfish, every now and again nodding in polite reply to something one of them had said.

Lady Thornton smiled with delight. The elderly lady was having a marvelous time, particularly since Lucy was the belle of the evening. Of course, this wasn't an official come-out, yet Lucy's success far surpassed even that of her dear Lillibet, and Lady Thornton knew her granddaughter's plans to start a school for young ladies would be moot by tomorrow afternoon, for surely there would be at least one proposal, if not two, as a result of this night.

"I say, Miss Wickham, won't you allow me to get you another piece of marzipan or a fruit tart?" Lord Wyatt inquired when Lucy's plate was empty, and before she might reply, the young gentleman was out of his seat and headed toward the buffet table in her behalf.

Lord Wyatt's departure afforded Lord Burnham Lucy's undivided attention, whereupon he launched into a detailed account of the stud at Burnham Manor. Did she know the last four champions on the heath at Newmarket had been from his stud? One could tell from the coloring, you know. Deep roan with a touch of cream on the forehead. Of course, the legs were notable as well; the animals had been bred for speed and it showed in the legs. This was a deathly boring discourse, and Lucy's mind drifted.

She'd been thinking about the earl all night, the cool touch of the ruby necklace a constant reminder of him, and everything Lady Bronwen had said kept repeating over and over in her mind. *Remember, this need not be a farewell ball.* Oh, if only that could be true, but any sort of conversation with the earl seemed impossible since they were never in the same room for more than a few moments. When she'd entered the rotunda after her conversation with Lady Bronwen, he'd gone off to talk with Captain Pomeroy; he had spent, she assumed from his absence, most of his time in the card room; and when she'd entered the long gallery and seen him again, he'd gone out to the terrace without so much as a nod in her direction. Why, if what Lady Bronwen claimed about the rubies was true, did he seem to be avoiding her?

Although she wasn't sure what she intended to say, Lucy bid her grandmother and Lord Burnham a polite adieu, and when no one was looking, she slipped between the draperies to join the earl on the terrace.

A brief line of light fell across the terrace, and the earl turned from his regard of the gardens. His face was in darkness, but his low voice encouraged Lucy to join him by the balcony railing.

"Are you enjoying yourself?" he asked.

The moon came out from behind a cloud. There was a rather wolfish smile upon his face, and Lucy couldn't resist offering a flirtatious little grin. "Yes, very much, although I'm not used to so much attention."

"You must get used to it. Beautiful ladies are always the center of attention. Did you know you look like a princess?" he asked in a velvety whisper.

Lucy blushed. This wasn't the first time someone had called her princess. All those years at the Royal Brighton Academy she had been called

Princess, but despite the appellation and the material abundance she had enjoyed, she'd never felt like a princess until this moment. There was a fullness of affection in the way the name rolled off the earl's lips, causing her heart to melt and her pulse to quicken. Finding herself somewhat tongue-tied, she said the first thing that popped into her head. "The first time I saw Clovelly I thought it looked like a fairy-tale palace."

"Ah, then you are in your rightful setting," was his reply, so soft and tender it was more of a caress than spoken word. He reached out and touched her cheek. The back of his right hand rested against her jaw, his fingertips brushing her lips. He whispered, "I should like to kiss you. You know that, don't you?"

Lucy could scarcely breathe, no less utter a reply to this beguiling question. Her lips tingled, and her knees were unsteady. She forced herself not to look away from his intense regard, and somehow she managed a nod.

"And would you like that?" was his enticing query. "Would you like me to kiss you?"

Her tongue darted out to moisten dry lips, and she had to swallow before she could speak. "Yes," she said, hardly recognizing her own voice. It was breathy and hoarse.

"You must come closer," he murmured. His right hand moved from where it rested against her cheek to cup the back of her head, and his other hand went to her waist to pull her into an embrace.

She nodded once more, as if to give consent to this sudden intimacy. His muscular thighs were pressed against her legs, his heart beat against her breast, and he was warm and hard from head to toe. There was something irresistible about being so close to him. It was frightening, too, and Lucy shivered as some sixth sense told her these sensations were mere prelude to what could happen between a man and a woman.

She made up her mind then. Even if the earl didn't love her, she wanted his kiss more than anything. She didn't want to look back on this evening and wonder what if . . .

Willingly, Lucy turned within his embrace, and acting on instinct, her arms went about his shoulders, her hands threaded through his long black hair, and her mouth angled upward to meet his. How long she stood within his embrace and how long they kissed would always remain a mystery to Lucy. Her most vivid memory would be of his strength, so tenderly controlled, and the way his gently moving lips revealed a depth of yearning she had never dreamed possible.

She whispered in the tiny space between them, ''No one's ever kissed me like that before.''

''Not even Anthony?''

''Not even Anthony.'' Her voice was dreamy, heavy with newly awakened passion. ''No one has ever made me feel like this before.''

''And how is that? How do I make you feel?''

''Warm and tingly and filled with expectation. It's as if something monumental is going to happen to me, and although I ought to be frightened, I'm not because I'm with you. No matter what happens it will be all right.''

''What do you think it means, Lucy?'' he asked on a husky underbreath.

''I think it means . . .'' She was about to say ''I love you,'' but the words stuck in her throat. An almost palpable fear of rejection, after having once before lost this man, rose out of this moment of fiery ardor and overwhelmed Lucy. Dread and apprehension took control and prevented her from speaking the truth.

"Yes, Lucy? Tell me what it means," he coaxed, noting the trembling in her lips and the tears in her eyes. His heart contracted at her confusion. Softly, very softly, he asked, "Why do you think I gave you the rubies?"

No other question could have so quickly vanquished her fierce apprehension. It was like a miracle. His reference to the rubies told Lucy all she needed to know, and there could be no doubt that the twins and the dowager countess had spoken the truth. The earl loved her, and there was no reason to hold back the truth another moment longer. Before Lucy could stop herself, she smiled, a delicate and impish gesture, not unlike the grin of the carefree child she had once been.

On a light ripple of laughter, she said, "I think I'd like to marry you, sir, if you please."

The present swirled away, and it was as if they were standing on that beach in Sussex once again.

"Was that a proposal?" he asked, his deep voice husky with emotion.

"Indeed, sir. Will you marry me?" Lucy reached up to the earl's face and as she had dreamed of doing, she took off the black patch. It fell to the flagstone terrace, and she gazed into his eyes, deep blue forging with green in a blaze of passion. She smiled again, flirtatious and beguiling. "Although the prospect of being a pirate's bride has always tantalized me, you look much better like this."

The earl tossed back his head and laughed, full and free and whole. "I should have said yes to your proposal all those years ago . . . damn to the gossips. I should have taken you away from that academy and sent you to live with my mother until you were old enough and the time was right."

"Am I old enough now?" was her tempting query.

He surveyed the fullness of her breasts, the slender waist, and those ever so kissable lips. Looking like he might devour her on the spot, he gave a roguish grin and nodded. "Quite perfect."

Her heart raced. She was breathless. "And is the time right?"

Once more, his lips descended to hers. He murmured, "When there is love, my sweet minx, the time is always right."

L'Envoi
❀ ❀ ❀ ❀

S EVEN MONTHS LATER the Earl and Countess
of Harrow stood at the top of the mauve
horseshoe staircase and watched as three carriages wheeled down the drive. Lady Bronwen
and Lady Thornton rode in the first coach, chattering as they went, reminding one another of the
two thousand details still unattended regarding
the upcoming semester at Mottistone Academy;
the ladies were bound for Lymington and the
ferry to Yarmouth on the Isle of Wight. In the
second carriage, Edith shared a seat with a cousin
of Miss Somerville-Large, who had been engaged
as a chaperon; they were destined for Captain
Pomeroy's family seat in Buckinghamshire. And
the third vehicle bore an exhilarated Eglantine,
who sat upon the edge of her seat, listening most
attentively to the Dowager Duchess of Exeter's
description of her goddaughters' roles as patronesses of Almack's; their final destination was Exeter House on Berkeley Square, Mayfair.

"I can hardly believe they're gone," said Lucy
when the line of vehicles disappeared from sight.
She linked an arm through her husband's as they
entered the house.

"You don't sound very pleased." Gazing down

205

at Lucy, the earl offered a roguish grin. "And here I was thinking that you'd be thrilled to have me all to yourself."

"Oh, Alex, you know I am." She hugged his arm and angled her head to kiss him on the cheek.

"Then why aren't you smiling?"

"It seems so quiet, and they've scarcely been gone ten minutes." Their footsteps echoed through the corridor. "Ever since my arrival, Clovelly has been teeming with activity. The notion of solitude seems strange. Besides, you know how much I love having family about, and I shall miss every single one of them most dreadfully."

"Don't tell me you married me for my family," he declared in mock horror. He feigned a wounded expression. "And all along I thought you'd been captivated by my piratical splendor."

Lucy laughed as she looked into his beautiful sea-blue eyes. How happy she'd been when he'd discarded the eye patch for good. As always his gaze was ablaze with love and the promise of passion. Rather breathless, she replied, "You mustn't tease me, Alex. You know perfectly well what I mean."

"Of course I do, and they'll be back soon. Sooner than I'd wish," he added on a husky undertone. One hand stroked her cheek in a way that quickly changed from comforting to seductive. "You know they won't be able to stay away for long. Anyway, sweet minx, we'll soon have a little family of our own to populate Clovelly, and then you'll find yourself wondering if it was ever quiet." He gazed at her waistline, and while one hand cupped her chin, the other splayed out across her gently rounding stomach.

Lucy sighed. "I suppose I should appreciate the quiet while it lasts."

"Clever girl." He dropped a tender kiss on her upturned lips and they continued down the corridor.

"What's this?" They had entered the rotunda and a package wrapped in silver foil caught Lucy's attention. There was a card. "It's for us, from Eglantine, and she says: 'I hope you enjoy this little something special to help you remember your first year together at Clovelly.' "

It was a scrapbook, and Lucy and Alex took it to the library, where they sat in a window seat and opened to the first carefully pasted page.

"Double agent apprehended!" began the clipping from the *Times,* which detailed the capture of the notorious double agent Henri Justin Blackmere, who had assumed the persona of the mild-mannered Mr. Pratt. Beginning with a lurid litany of Blackmere's crimes against the Crown, the article concluded with a vivid commentary of the midsummer gala at Clovelly Priory, Dorset, where the spy had been identified by the gallant Captain Pomeroy and his escape had been foiled by the captain with the assistance of the courageous Lady Edith Paget, niece of the Earl of Harrow.

"Do you remember how Eglantine cried?" remarked Lucy.

"How could I forget? She kept the entire household awake for a sennight with her wailing. Though I must say her gravest disappointment was not Mr. Pratt's treachery but the fact there wasn't a single mention of her name in print. Do you think she's recovered?"

"Quite, though had she not, I believe these next few weeks under the dowager duchess's tutelage shall do the trick. She's grown into quite a beauty and is surely to be one of the Season's Incomparables."

"Perhaps there shall even be a betrothal?"

"Indeed." Lucy nodded, then turned to the next page and smiled as her eyes rested upon a variety of items announcing the September marriage of Miss Lucy Wickham to Alexander Paget, the Earl of Harrow. The couple had been wed in the private chapel at Aylesbury, and the bride, contrary to etiquette and tradition, had been attended by her grandmother, Lady Thornton, and her great-aunt, the Dowager Duchess of Mitford.

One of the formal wedding invitations, italics on ecru vellum bordered in gold, was pasted to the fourth page; on the fifth page, there appeared a small item from the socials column of the Weymouth paper which noted that the newlywed couple had spent several weeks sailing along the coast. That same column also remarked upon the extraordinary fine health of the Dowager Countess of Harrow.

"Mother did make a miraculous recovery," remarked the earl in such a tone of skepticism that Lucy was taken aback.

"Alex, you're not implying that she . . . that she—"

"Faked her entire illness," he supplied for her. "Indeed, I am. Did you never find it rather peculiar and more than a bit of a coincidence that she was near death's door one day, but quite well enough to hostess a gala shortly thereafter?"

"Well, yes, but—"

"There, you see, we're in agreement," the earl stated as he turned the page and nearly choked at the next item he saw. "Egad, how in heaven's name did Eglantine get a hold of this little souvenir?" he exclaimed.

"What is it?" Lucy peered at the clipping on

the next page. It appeared to have come from some sort of ledger.

"I don't believe it, but it looks like a page from the betting book at White's. Yes, indeed, it is. See, here you have the date and the member's name, followed by his wager. I quite recognize the numbering in the upper left-hand corner. This is extraordinary. Absolutely extraordinary."

"But what ever are they betting on?"

"Dalsany, it appears. The first of the wagers are dated two days after our wedding, and they appear to be speculating upon his future security. Baldwin, Palmerston, and Drummond each bet twenty pounds Anthony would be shipped off to Botany Bay for his debts; and the remainder, a good dozen or more, put their money on the eventuality that he'd fall upon the good graces of the Dowager Duchess of Exeter and be back in Town and up to his usual tricks before All Hallows."

"But he confounded them all when he eloped to Gretna Green with Lady Priscilla Fox Strangways."

"Indeed, and continues to confound them, for they're very particular about keeping these books in order, and I'm sure no one can imagine what happened to this page."

"Do you think he took it?"

"Knowing his vanity, there's no doubt he did. And then he probably flaunted it before Eglantine, who decided it would be a clever addition to this collection."

Lucy couldn't help laughing. "Anthony always did amuse me. Perhaps you should place a wager on its whereabouts."

"And catapult poor Anthony into another social broth? I believe Lady Priscilla and her parents are trouble enough for him.''

A tiny frown crossed Lucy's brow. ''I can't help feeling a bit sorry for him, you know.''

''You always did have a kind heart, my dear minx.''

''Is there nothing we can do for them? I know you've been more than generous with Anthony and infinitely patient, but Lady Priscilla is as profligate as Anthony and now that she's been disowned, I quite fear for them.''

The earl smiled at his wife. ''Were it not for you I might actually let them stew in this mess of their own making, but knowing how you would feel I've decided to send Anthony to the Paget plantation in the Caribbean. It's not a bad life. The house is lovely, the neighbors are educated and more cosmopolitan than you'd imagine. He'll be lord of the manor and with some hard work and a few good crops, they should be quite wealthy in their own right.''

''Thank you, dearest Alex,'' she whispered between a series of light kisses to his strong, warm lips. The familiar scent of cloves comforted her, and she snuggled closer to her husband. ''I knew you were not as coldhearted as you would like the rest of us to imagine.''

The next few pages in the scrapbook were comprised of invitations to various parties in the surrounding Dorset countryside, including the revived hunt ball at Aylesbury.

At Christmas, Captain Pomeroy visited Clovelly, and there was a ceremony in his honor at the assembly rooms in Weymouth, an event which was fully described in the local paper.

Several weeks into the new year, there was an announcement in the *Times* of Captain Pomeroy's betrothal to Lady Edith Paget; a June wedding at St. George's, Mayfair, was planned. That clipping was pasted across from an announcement signed by Lady Bronwen and Lady Thornton apprising Society of the opening of Mottistone Academy. Owing to the aristocratic rank of the founders, enrollment at Mottistone was soon full, and fifteen young ladies, ranging in ages from nine to twelve, had been students at Mottistone for the past five months.

"My mother never ceases to amaze me," remarked the earl after rereading the announcement for the umpteenth time. He would always remember the moment his mother had brought a copy to him and told him of her plans to quit Clovelly and accompany Lady Thornton to the Isle of Wight. "Had you suggested a year ago that she would found a school for young ladies I would never have believed it."

"But then your mother has always been in charge, even as a young girl in her father's home, and now that the twins are gone I think she knew she would miss the challenge of molding young ladies. And, of course, she never tired of saying that my grandmother was far too old to be embarking upon such an undertaking on her own, so I'm sure she means to be in charge of her as well."

"You're quite right, and I do think Mother savored some secret rush of excitement that she had managed to set Society upon its ear with her announcement."

Lucy giggled. "Imagine how Society shall react upon learning swimming has supplanted needlework in the education of proper young ladies."

"Mayhap Society shall balk, but I've no fear enrollment at the academy will suffer. I wager my mother and your grandmother will have no trouble whatsoever convincing their students' parents of the wisdom of such a progressive curriculum. Although I've never liked the notion of packing girls off to school, I think our daughter would find a boarding school experience at Mottistone most pleasurable."

"What do you mean by 'our daughter'?" There was a touch of indignation in Lucy's question. "This child is a son, and your heir, sir."

"I would be happy with either, dear minx. Besides, we've plenty of time for more babies," he murmured suggestively.

A furious blush colored Lucy's cheeks.

"Oh, that I might be able to read your mind. That blush is most enticing," he whispered as his lips burned a trail of kisses from her brow, down one cheek, and along her jaw. "Tell me, dear minx, do you think of me?"

The husky quality in his voice and the promise of his kisses caused Lucy's heart to beat faster. "I was thinking how happy you've made me, and how incredible it is that I love you more with each passing day."

"Ah, then you would not be averse to populating every room in Clovelly?"

"Not in the least," she replied as she surrendered to his kiss.

The scrapbook slid to the floor, and the final page was forgotten. It featured a missive from the Dowager Duchess of Exeter to Lady Bronwen, formally offering to sponsor Lady Eglantine in London.

It is my intention to make Lady Eglantine the belle of the Season and to insure that she contract the most advantageous match in the realm. She is, after all, my dear brother's granddaughter, and as her twin is already affianced, I could do no less than to insure Lady Eglantine's future security. Perhaps, the Earl of Cheke, although a bit of a rake, would be suitable; I've known his mother for years, his bloodlines are impeccable, and while he's managed to avoid matrimony for several years I know he must soon populate a nursery. Or perhaps the Corinthian, Sir John Gatcombe, would interest Lady Eglantine. Sir John owns vast estates in the south and north, and his wife would be one of the wealthiest ladies in the realm. Then there is Viscount Rookley, a distant relative of my late husband's, and although the youngest of the three, I believe he's no less handsome or financially secure. Young Eglantine could do no worse than to select from three such eligible gentlemen.

And that, dear reader, is quite another story.

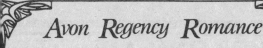